MARCH
TOWARD THE
THUNDER

by JOSEPH BRUCHAC

SCHOLASTIC INC.
New York Toronto London Auckland
Sydney Mexico City New Delhi Hong Kong

ISBN: 978-0-545-23426-9

12 11 10 9 8 7 6 5 4 3 2 1   9 10 11 12 13 14/0

Printed in the U.S.A.   40

First Scholastic printing, December 2009

Text set in Meridien
Designed by Kimi Weart

The map of Virginia (on page v) originally appeared in the May 4, 1861 edition of *Harper's Weekly* newspaper.

For our grandchildren;
may they live to see
a world in which
there is no war

Old Virginia,
the Heartland of the Civil War

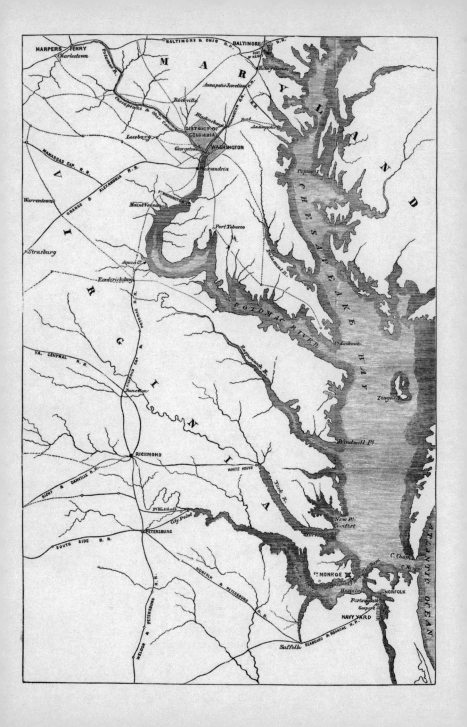

As he lay in the stinking mud of the trench outside Petersburg, Louis thought about what had brought him there.

The money?

More greenbacks than a boy of his age could ever hope to earn—especially one who was just an Indian. Cash enough to buy good clothing for his mother, even a horse to carry her loads so that her feet might not ache so much at the end of a long day of walking the road into town. A thick enough stack of the new paper dollars to buy a little piece of land that would be their own, so that no one again could order them to leave their camp like common vagrants. On such land he could even one day raise a family. And as he thought of that, the image of Azonis's sweet face briefly came to him and made him smile.

Yes, the money made such a future possible. But it wasn't just *the money that brought him to this killing field. No more than it was just the trail that brought the deer within range of the hunters' guns.*

The insults?

He thought back on the gang of boys who'd met M'mere and him as the two of them tried to slip into town, loaded down with sacks full of baskets.

"Gypsies, dirty Indian gypsies!" the tallest boy yelled at them, his face twisted with contempt.

"Go back where yuh come from, yuh blamed tramps," shouted a fat-faced redhead. He bent, picked up a potato-sized cobble and threw it. It would have struck his mother if Louis hadn't shielded her with his body and felt the stone bounce off his own broad back. He clenched a fist.

"Non." Marie Nolette, his gentle mother, grasped his sleeve with her healing hands, palms rough and scarred from many seasons of weaving ash withes into baskets. "Patience. Nous aller. *They will grow tired of this game."*

Although she was trying to hold him back, even though there were six or seven in the mob, he was about to take his mother's walking stick and wade into them. They were likely about his age, fourteen, fifteen, but none of them as big as he.

But before Louis could get hold of that stick, something else caught the eyes and ears of the boys. The flash of blue cloth and the glint of oiled metal. The thump of a drum and the measured tramp of feet.

"It's our boys in blue!"

"Soldiers!"

And, just like that, the gang of boys turned and ran off after the squad of marching men who'd just turned the corner a block away. By the time they reached the soldiers, the boys had dropped their stones and replaced them with sticks held up to their shoulders in imitation of the .58-caliber Model 1861 Rifle Muskets carried by the new recruits. Each and every man was dressed in a blue flannel thigh-length sack coat and blue wool trousers, a slouch cap perched on his head, chin held high and proud.

"Kill some Rebs for us, sir."

"Take it to them Sessesh snakes!"

As those neatly uniformed marching men and the boys who copied them went around the corner and out of sight, they all began to sing.

"We'll hang Jeff Davis from a sour apple tree!

We'll hang Jeff Davis from a sour apple tree!"

It was a stirring song. But what Louis remembered most were those fine, clean uniforms.

In a uniform like theirs, *Louis thought,* I would not look like either a ragged gypsy or a dirty Indian.

CHAPTER ONE

HEAR THAT

Saturday, April 2, 1864

"*Kina?*" Marie Nolette said, her head lifted like a deer sniffing the air. "Hear that?"

Her voice was soft. Most people wouldn't have heard her speak, since hooves and wagon wheels clattered on the cobblestones of Broadway. Dozens of people were talking as they passed along the sidewalk. It was a busy Saturday morning in front of the hotel where she and Louis were carefully placing their ash splint baskets on display.

Louis Nolette, though, was used to paying attention to his mother's quiet voice.

"Ayup," he replied.

How could he not have heard that deep rumble? It was a hundred times louder than the wheels of a heavy wagon over the plank road that led out of town toward their camp north of the village. It came not from nearby nor from the earth, but from above. It was the distant voice of Bedagi, the ancient thunder being. In the stories of long ago, before the coming of the white men, Bedagi's arrows of lightning destroyed the monsters that threatened his people.

But Louis knew that what his mother had said was not just about hearing the thunder. It was about its meaning. Far-off thunder might mean danger was near.

The deep rumble came again. It touched something inside the broad-shouldered boy as he stood there, muscular arms full of the baskets they'd made. Old Bedagi was walking the sky somewhere above the Kaydeross Range to the north of the town. Maybe he was looking down now from the clouds over the swamps by Ireland Vly where Louis had found the black ash trees for these baskets.

Papa, Louis thought, *you taught me well. I have not forgotten one bit. I know how to find the right trees, how to thank them properly before cutting them. I remember how to use the heavy club to pound along the peeled ash trunk as it is on the ground. Tunk-tunk tunk, tunk-tunk tunk. Two strikes forward, then one back. My arms have grown stronger doing this work.*

To do it right you had to move slowly down the length of the peeled log, breaking the fibers in between the seasonal ring so that the withes would lift up to be pulled free. Thin rings were laid down in times of drought, thicker ones in seasons when the rains were good and steady.

Louis nodded. *Spring thunder is also a good sound. Rains coming. Soon everything will turn green and grow in the moons of planting and hoeing that lay ahead. Maybe in this year of our Lord, 1864, me and M'mere will earn enough to buy a few acres.*

There was a chance of that. They had been making a little more money this spring. Not just from their baskets, but also from his mother's doctoring and birthing.

They'd only been camping in the area for three months, but word had spread about "Aunt Marie, the Abenaki doctoress." Country folk hereabouts had learned that Marie Nolette was the best to call upon for certain things, especially the way she understood what to do when a mother's time came to bring her child into the light of day.

Not only that, M'mere, she knows when the need for her is great. She shows up at the door of some farm far from town just when some frantic husband, he is about to send for help.

More often than not these days, though, it was a worried mother-in-law and not a husband. So many men were off to war, lonely wives having babies who might never see their fathers' faces.

Louis quickly turned his thoughts away from children whose fathers were gone.

M'mere, she is a healer, as well.

It didn't matter if it was a broken limb or a burn or even one of those deep wounds that so often happened to people when they were doing farm work around plows and pitchforks and scythes. Or if someone had a deep hacking cough, she would know what tea to make—from the needles of the white pine, perhaps—to clear away catarrh. Aunt Marie, everyone said, held the way to treat just about every injury or ailment one could imagine—short of bringing a person back from the dead.

Not every family could afford to pay her cash. Sometimes she might be given food or used clothes rather than the few coins a poor family might scrape together. But other times, knowing Marie and her son as basket-makers, a family would grant them permission to go into their woodlot and take any of the black ash that grew where the soil was moist. Louis had marked more than fifty such trees to be cut when the season was right.

Louis nodded to himself as he put the last of the baskets down. Yes, in another year or two they might earn enough to put down a payment on a little farm. There was good land hereabouts to buy—more than usual. Many acres went unplowed these days with such a multitude of men off to the conflict and so many never coming home again.

Louis looked down at the newspaper. It had been dropped on the sidewalk by a dandy who'd spent a good bit of time eyeing their baskets without buying a one. It wasn't the swells who usually bought baskets from them, but ordinary folks who used them around the home. At least he'd left that paper for Louis to read.

Louis prided himself on his ability to read in both English and French. In their old home up in Canada, he and his parents had always mixed languages together. Sometimes they spoke in Abenaki, sometimes in French, sometimes even a little English. It was a wise thing to know languages. Like most other Indians, they traveled from place to place to make their living. One season might be spent in the lands to the south where only English was heard, another among the Quebecois who refused to speak anything other than their beloved French. Even more than most other Abenakis, Louis had a gift for languages.

When he was a schoolboy at St. Francis he'd often been praised by the nuns who were his teachers. He'd also been an altar boy. Father Andre tried to talk him into going into the priesthood. When he told his parents about the old priest's idea, they looked at each other and then back at their son.

"The Father," Louis said, "he assures me that I will make a fine priest."

That resulted in another long silence.

"What do you think, my son?" his father finally asked.

"I think," Louis replied, keeping his voice as serious as possible, "it is likely to happen . . ."—he paused—"when fish turn into birds and fly south for the winter."

Louis smiled at how he and his parents had laughed on that day. Back then, when he was eleven winters old, his ambition was to be just like his father. He would hunt and trap, make baskets. When they needed cash money, he would do as his father did every other year—travel south to work as a logger.

That same autumn day when he teased his parents about

becoming a priest, his father and other men from St. Francis left for lumber camp in Maine. Papa promised he would return in the spring after the drive down the Kennebec.

"Look for me after the first *tonnerre*. I'll be back with ribbons for your hair, *mon femme*, and a new *fusil* for you, *mon fils*."

What came to them after that first thunder, though, was not his beloved father. It was word that Jean Nolette drowned during the drive down the Kennebec. He'd been buried on a hill above the bend in the river where he'd lost his life.

Four winters had passed since his father left them. It still seemed as if it was just yesterday. Some mornings Louis woke up certain he would see his father coming down the trail with that new rifle for his son slung over his shoulder.

Louis had to turn his thoughts away from that memory. He stared at the front page of the newspaper at his feet. News of the war. Since it began three years ago he'd followed every development in the struggle between the North—which seemed to him to have the right on their side seeing as how they were going against slave-holders—and the South.

"Their fight, not ours," his mother said over his shoulder.

Louis nodded, hardly hearing her. His mother spoke those same words more often. She worried about the way his eyes grew faraway each time he read of the Union Army's heroic struggles. Accounts of battles held a fascination for him like nothing else.

Louis did notice, though, how newspapers were printing good news again. Everything was going fine. It'd been that way when war was declared in '61 after the firing on Sumter.

Papers and men on the street swore it'd all be over in a month, maybe two. The Sesseshes would crawl back into the Union like whipped puppies, tails between their legs.

Then came Bull Run. General McDowell's invincible Union Army went out to face the outnumbered Confederates for what most folks expected to be a lark. Ladies and gents and members of Congress drove their coaches out to where the battle was to take place, spread blankets out on the hills, brought out picnic lunches. Northern troops in their new uniforms stopped to pick the ripe blackberries gleaming along the Virginia roadsides that twenty-first day of July.

But General Pierre G. T. Beauregard and his Confederate boys had plans of their own that didn't include picnics or turning tail. The day ended with 2,900 Union soldiers dead or wounded. It was only because the Rebs took 2,000 casualties of their own that they hadn't just marched right in and taken over Washington.

Since then there'd been too many bloody battles to count. Shiloh, Second Bull Run, Antietam, Chancellorsville, Gettysburg. Those were the ones Louis remembered best from the news accounts. He'd been both thrilled and horrified. On the one hand, it made him glad that he was safe and far away from battle. But he couldn't help but wonder.

Me, would I measure up to be a soldier?

The war was still going on, but the papers declared that the Southern cause was doomed. Only the Copperheads—those fool Southern sympathizers with their calls for peace at any price—saw things differently. Arkansas and Louisiana were back in the Union fold. Gettysburg had been a great Union victory. With General Ulysses S. Grant in charge, the reins were in the hands of the North. But there were still thousands of men coming home in boxes or limping back so badly wounded they'd be crippled-up for the rest of their days.

Louis's eye was caught by a piece farther down the page. The United States Senate had passed a joint resolution on April 8 approving the Thirteenth Amendment by a vote of 38 to 6. The Emancipation Proclamation, which President Lincoln issued back in 1862, was finally going to be ratified.

Louis wondered about that.

Why'd it take so long for the Union to free the slaves? Why was there slavery in the first place?

Back in Canada slavery had long been outlawed. That was why the runaway Negroes headed there.

How can one man own another?

It made no sense. Nor did it make sense that so many white people in the "free states" still owned slaves. From what Louis heard, even General Grant's wife owned a slave or two. Some said the war wasn't about slavery but about the right of states to do what they pleased. That too didn't make sense to Louis.

Am I too young to understand these things? He shook his head. *I've only seen fifteen winters, but it seems to me that slavery's what the battle ought be about.*

A war to free the slaves—that touched his spirit. Louis had met some escaped slaves in Canada. They were dark-skinned men and women and children who traveled at night toward the winter land, following the star shape Louis knew as the Great Bear—though they called it the Drinking Gourd. They'd stop by the Nolette camp on the river and stay the night, grateful for the good vittles the serious-faced Indian boy (his skin only a shade lighter than theirs) and his gentle mother shared.

It wasn't unusual that he and his mother helped those run-aways. Most Indians didn't hesitate to make a place by the fire for any fugitive who needed a bed for the night and a bite of food. After all, Abenakis knew what it was to run for their lives.

Before his great-grandparents came to Canada, they'd lived in Ndakinna, their old homeland now named Vermont and New Hampshire. If they hadn't fled, they might have been killed like so many other Indians back then. Wave after wave of Englishmen swept in, washing over the hills, turning Native land into New England. Those English even turned some captured Indians into slaves—like those darker-skinned men and women they later brought from across the ocean.

Louis shook his head. He didn't like thinking about such things—neither the bringing of slaves nor the sad day when their allies the French gave up their long war against the English and left the Indians on their own to fight or die, hide in the hills or retreat.

The thunder rumbled again, closer than it had been before.

"Sounds a bit like cannon fire, does it not, young fellow?" said a voice from his left.

CHAPTER TWO
THE RECRUITER

Saturday, April 2, 1864

Louis didn't look up. He'd sensed the white man standing there, but had not acknowledged him. He didn't look the sort who'd pay attention to a pair of basket sellers. He was far too well-dressed to be a farmer or even a merchant. Tall beaver hat and that silk vest, watch chain hanging out of it. With those polished boots and that cane in his hand, he seemed too full of himself to be buying a basket. But why else would he stoop to talk to a brown-skinned young man?

Unless a white man wanted to buy from you or hire you or you were in his way and he expected you to step aside, there was no reason for a gentleman dressed like a lawyer to take notice of an Indian boy.

His mother pointedly paid no attention to the man. She focused on their baskets, arranging them on the long pole. They didn't have a sign out. The baskets were sign enough. Plus most of their customers knew them, seeing as how they were here five days a week. Folks had learned that a Nolette basket was woven tight and strong.

"A good basket can outlive the hand that made it," his mother often said.

Ash is tough and it holds on, Louis thought, *as we do*.

You might pound on ash to raise the rings from the trunk and pull off the withes, but it stayed strong as sinew. A thin strip of ash could hold the weight of a man if you looped it over a limb.

The man cleared his throat.

"Good morning, young man," he said. Something in the tone of his voice made Louis pay attention. The man wasn't just being polite. He wanted something.

No need to talk when talking is not needed.

So his father, Jean, used to say. It was now Louis's motto. Two fingers held up meant the basket cost twenty cents. A nod or a shake of the head was all that was needed to transact the sale after that. More than one person who bought from them went away thinking Louis and his mother spoke no English at all.

But this might be their first sale of the day. Saying something could make a difference. So Louis used his best English, not even a trace of a French accent in it.

"Good morning, sir," he replied.

Only three words, but they earned Louis more than he'd bargained for.

"Ah," the man said, showing his teeth in a broad grin that looked more hungry than friendly. "You speak English."

"Yes, sir."

"Excellent! I thought that might be so when I saw you studying that newspaper. You can read as well, can't you?"

"I can," Louis answered, his voice a little slower this time.

This conversation, where is it leading?

"So you have been following the fortunes of our valiant lads in this great War for Abolition, this Struggle Against Slavery."

Louis's mother was no longer arranging her baskets. She moved next to her son and grasped him by the elbow. He knew what that meant. But he ignored the touch on his arm that meant he should end this conversation.

"You could say that," Louis replied. More words than needed. *Why am I trying to prove that I speak English as well as a white man?*

"Indeed." The man's smile was so broad now that you could count his teeth. It made Louis think of a picture he'd seen once in a book. A big-mouthed, sharp-toothed thing called a crocodile. "Might I ask what sort of work you do, lad?"

So that is what this is about. He is just looking to hire an able-bodied man.

"Mostly I'm a common laborer," Louis said, beginning to feel relieved.

"Excellent! And how old might you be?"

The kind of question a stranger ought not to ask. His mother tugged at his arm again. But Louis saw no harm in answering. "Just turned fifteen, sir."

The man looked disappointed. For half a heartbeat the crocodile smile slipped from his face. He stroked his broad chin with the long thumb of the skinny clawlike hand that held the cane.

"Fifteen, fifteen," the man said in a musing tone. "But big enough."

The grin reappeared as he turned his attention again to Louis. "Why, there's young men half your size wearing the blue. You could pass for twenty."

Louis shook his head. "I am not that old."

"A mere technicality, lad. They'll take you at your word, what with the losses they've . . ." The man paused. "I mean to say, what with the need of the brigade at present, seeing as how so many have served and are being allowed to go home now. Which is why I have been employed to assist the good Captain Forsythe in his efforts. But I am putting the cart ahead of the horse, eh?"

Louis tried to picture a wagon being pushed by a horse. It didn't make a lick of sense. Then again, little of what this man with the big teeth had said amounted to anything that Louis could understand. But he kept his peace, even though he sensed the man was waiting for his reply.

Some men, they are great talkers. Keeping quiet, that encourages others to talk—maybe even more than if you say something. Why waste your breath asking a question when you can get the answer by holding your tongue?

"Ah," the man said, trying another tack. "I see, my boy, that you are a thinker. Do you know what this war is really about? Our fight is to preserve the Union."

If it is your fight, why are you not carrying a gun into battle? Why are you standing here and jawing at me?

The man saw that question in Louis's eyes. "If I were a young lad like you, I'd be the first to sign up." He sighed. "But alas, my health is too poor for me to serve in the ranks." He hooked his long thumbs into his vest and took a deep breath. "I'll put it to you plain, my boy. How would you like to strike a blow to preserve our beloved nation?"

Louis couldn't keep himself from answering that one. "It is not my nation, sir," he said. "M'mere and me, we are from Canada. We are Indians."

His mother, who'd been hovering over his shoulder, smiled at that. She turned back to her baskets, certain the conversation was now over.

To Louis's surprise, though, the man in the tall hat didn't look discouraged. If anything, the man's reptilian grin did what Louis would have thought impossible a moment before—it actually got broader.

"Son," the man said, placing a well-manicured hand on Louis's shoulder, "let me get right to the point. Apart from patriotism to spur you on, there are further incentives. For one, you'd receive a fine new uniform, much better than those rough-spun clothes you are wearing now. Made of fine cloth, none of that shoddy material what was so callously handed out to our troops early on in the war. You'll get new boots, as well. And your very own rifle will be issued, nothing less than a fine percussion muzzleloader, the Model 1861 Rifle Musket."

At the talk of the uniform and the gun, Louis had started to take more notice, but the man was not yet finished. His best point was still to come—as the hand gesture he made, a bony finger lifted dramatically to point toward the sky, indicated. He leaned toward Louis, lowered his voice.

"Also," the man whispered, "there's the bounties. Not only a one-hundred-dollar federal enlistment bonus—payable on signing—but our grand state of New York's offering a five-hundred-dollar bounty for first-time enlistees. Moreover, each soldier will receive another seventy-five dollars at the end of the war, which will surely be soon. Then there's regular pay, a generous sixteen dollars per month. Promptly delivered into your hands by the government paymaster. Plus there is a pension for being wounded. Not that there would be much chance of that. Picket duty is about all a man might expect now."

"I will do it," a voice said.

To Louis's surprise, it was his own.

"I will join the army."

His mother turned Louis toward her and looked up into his eyes. She saw it there, the stubborn determination. So much like his father. Marie Nolette sighed as only a mother can.

Now that her brave and foolish son had spoken those words, there was no turning back.

CHAPTER THREE
NEW BLOOD

Friday, April 15, 1864

"'Tis a fine motley bunch ye are," the burly Irish sergeant growled as he walked down the line. "Not a man in the lot of ye worth the powder to blow ye to Kingdom Come. Straighten yer shoulders, lad!"

Louis tried to stand straighter, even though that comment was not meant for him but Private Merry to his left. Will Merry was not making much of a soldier thus far. He seemed determined, but didn't appear to have the stamina of the other men. Not surprising considering his size. Little Will was so short and slender that he looked even younger than Louis's own fifteen years.

Young as he was, Louis was taller, his shoulders broader than most of the other recruits. Several, like Merry, appeared to be under the legal age themselves. And though he'd discovered that he missed M'mere more than he'd expected, Louis was not one of those who cried out for his mama in his sleep—like the skinny farm boy behind him in the second rank, the one now nicknamed Possum.

What the other recruits had noticed, though, was the brown of his skin.

"You a mulatter or a Injun?"

He'd been asked that more than once after arriving at camp. Some spoke in a hostile tone, others seemed merely curious. To each he gave the same answer in a patient, neutral voice.

"Indian, Abenaki."

By the second day, no one still wondered if he was a light-skinned Negro. Word had gone round that they had a real Indian in their ranks.

Some of the men tried rough attempts at humor with him.

"Wouldn't you rather have a bow and arrer than that musket, Chief?"

"How come yer not wearin' feathers?"

"Not going to scalp us all in our sleep, are you?"

Louis showed no anger or resentment, hiding how he felt with a calm face. He gave no answer to such teasing jibes. After a few days, when it became clear that no response would be forthcoming, the teasing stopped.

————

The platoon had been at attention for so long that the sun had moved a hand's width higher in the early-morning sky. Louis's fingers that held the rifle at his side had almost gone numb. He flexed them to bring some feeling back. Letting his rifle drop was almost as bad as disobeying an order. No telling what they'd do to you then. He sure as shooting did not want to get punished the way Bull Belaney, who stood to his immediate right, had been disciplined just yesterday.

Belaney was muscled like a blacksmith and as broad as Will Merry was thin. He was also as mean-tempered as fair-haired Merry was eager and innocent. Trying to cheat at cards had led to Bull Belaney's punishment. When Merry objected that the big man had slipped a card from his boot, Bull knocked Merry down and lifted a foot to put the boot to him.

Sergeant Michael Flynn was nowhere to be seen until then.

Sergeant Flynn, he may be built like the bear, but he moves like the cat.

Belaney's boot never descended. Flynn appeared so fast to separate Bull from his prey, the bulky sergeant had seemed to materialize from thin air. That should have ended the matter. But Belaney took a swing at Flynn. The punch never connected. Belaney found himself on the ground with the sergeant's brogan wedged on the back of his neck.

"Ye think yerself t' be a fighting rooster?" Flynn rumbled. "'Tis time yer wings was clipped, then."

Belaney spent the afternoon propped against the flagpole,

hands tied, a wedge of wood in his mouth, a stout stick under his bent knees. He was kept like that until the bugle call for supper.

Belaney's bad attitude still remained, though. It showed itself so clearly that after less than a week in Camp Meagher every other recruit was steering clear of the man.

Trouble, it hangs around that one like a cloud.

Louis wondered why Bull Belaney had ever enlisted in the first place. Perhaps what some said about him was true—he was a bounty jumper. With so many greenbacks being offered now as enlistment bonuses to new recruits, a passel of scoundrels were making quick money by signing up under false names, collecting their bonuses, and then deserting to do it all again in another county.

But Sergeant Flynn, who accompanied them on the train from Troy all the way to Washington, marked Belaney from the start and kept a special eye on the man. He even followed whenever the man went to relieve himself.

Flynn, he has a way of looking into your eye and reading your mind.

Louis thought back to the first time he met Flynn. It was on the very day he enlisted.

Louis was nervous, but primed to repeat what Mr. Lemon told him to say. Lemon. That was the name of the lawyer in the tall hat who was also a state recruiting agent—justifying his claim to ten percent of the bounty paid to each recruit he brought in. Like a true attorney, he had ready answers for Louis's questions.

"Eighteen?" Louis asked. "How can I say that? Me, I am

three years shy of that. I cannot fit my mouth around a lie."

"No need to worry, my boy," Lemon assured him. "I have dealt with this, ah, issue before."

He reached into his vest pocket with a magician-like flourish to produce another card slightly larger than the first one he'd shown Louis, that read *George Lemon, Attorney at Law and Enlistment Agent*. Unlike the first card, which had been quickly returned to Lemon's pocket, that second card was left in Louis's hand.

"Use this, my boy, and all will be well."

"Are ye old enough t' serve?" the recruiting officer looked across the table into Louis's eyes.

Louis looked down.

Sergeant Michael Flynn, 69th New York Volunteers read the hand-lettered sign on the table.

"I am over eighteen," Louis carefully replied.

A little smile came onto the sergeant's face. "So," he exclaimed, "it's an honest one ye are, laddie? And 'tis the absolute truth that yer now telling me?"

"Yes, sir," Louis said, nodding his head.

"And wouldn't it be unfair of me, then, t' go on and ask if ye've not put some little piece of paper into yer shoe wit' the number eighteen writ large upon it?" Flynn quickly raised his palm. "No, ye need not answer that. It's just thinking out loud I am. We need all the new blood we can get and may God have mercy on our souls. Just sign yer name and welcome t' the service of Uncle Sam as a soldier in what is left of the Sixty-ninth, the finest regiment in the grandest of all the brigades that have ever been a part of the blessed Union Army."

"ORDER ARMS!"

The command woke Louis out of his reverie. Without thinking, he lifted his rifle and swung it in front of him so that it slapped into the palm of his left hand. All down the line, other members of the training squad did the same.

"Grand!" Sergeant Flynn shouted. "That's better, lads. Yer looking almost like soldiers now. I swear by all the saints that when I get done with ye, 'tis soldiers ye all will be. Even you, Belaney—if that is yer name."

Although he knew he had to keep his face expressionless, Louis almost smiled at that.

CHAPTER FOUR
BUGLES AND MUSKETS

Friday, April 29, 1864

"*Oleohneh Ktsi Nwaskw, Merci Beaucoup Bon Dieu.*" So Papa began the blessing before each of their meals, hands clasped together and head bowed. Then his father, his mother, and Louis would each raise a hand to touch forehead, chest, left shoulder and right, the sign of the cross where the Son of God suffered and died for all—even the Abenakis.

Those four points of the cross were also the four sacred directions, the dawn land that brings light to each new day, the summer land, the land of the sunset, and the winter land, whose white snows mark the wisdom of winter, just as white hairs crown the head of an elder. For every ritual of the

Catholic Church, Louis had also learned from his parents some piece of the old wisdom, the way their ancestors understood the blessings and dangers of this world.

"Awasosis," his father said, speaking the nickname he'd used for him ever since Louis was two winters old and had proven that he could climb a tree as well as a bear cub, "hold tight to your paddle. Hard rapids ahead."

Louis looked up. Just a heartbeat ago they'd been about to share their morning meal. Now they were in a canoe? Himself in front, his mother in the middle, his father in the back, digging in his paddle. The roar of the Lachine Rapids was all around them. Papa was shouting. Louis could not make out his words.

Louis lifted his paddle. It was not wood, but hard steel. It had turned into a musket. As he drove it in, the weight of the gun pulled him out of the canoe and down into the water. The canoe sped past overhead. No longer in the water, it was flying across the sky. His parents looked down and waved. A wide-winged bird swooped down. A loon. As its feet touched the surface it began to call a series of notes as familiar now to Louis as the sounds of snoring from the five other men who slept an arm's length away. It was the high, piercing voice of . . . a bugle!

Reveille!

Louis sat up in his cot. The dream was still with him, but he knew where he was. It was their seventh and last day in Camp Meagher. They'd been rushed through training as swiftly as a canoe swept down a rough river. No inspection or drill today.

They were marching out as soon as breakfast was over.

I am a soldier now. I have been trained for war. So why do I still dream of my parents and miss them as if I were a little child?

The five other men in the tent with him were yawning and scratching.

"My stars, Chief, why'd they let us sleep so late?" said a joking voice from behind him.

Timmy Kirk, of course. His bunk was next to Louis's. Though he said he was twenty years old some days and twenty-one on others, Kirk was another who looked younger than Louis. His wit as sharp as his hatchet-like features, he turned everything into a jest. He'd earned the nickname Joker.

Late? Louis thought, rubbing his chest. *In a pig's eye.*

That bugle call had sounded before the birds were awake. Five a.m.

Louis shoved his socked feet into the boots that looked so alike he only knew left from right by the position he placed them in beside his bed last night. They almost fit. Better than many another soldier could say. After yanking his brogans from the pile, Louis had quickly traded with other recruits around him. As a result, he had a pair of gunboats—as Joker called them—neither so huge he had to stuff in newspapers like Merry or so small he could barely wedge in his feet.

Being outfitted meant grabbing what was on the top of each pile. Heaps of light blouses, thick flannel pullover shirts, sky blue trousers. Those pants still itched like the dickens, but that wasn't the worst of it. Even his underwear was wool! It couldn't have been scratchier if it had been sewn out of spruce needles. With the South's cotton out of reach, the North had no choice but to love wool. He adjusted his waistband. His pants were loose on him, but it was that way with everyone. Like the others in his company, he'd slept in his flannel shirt and wool trousers.

No one in the army ever seemed to take all their clothes off. Unless you went for a swim, you might go through the war without ever seeing another soldier naked, even the man you shared your two-person field tent with. The only bathing a soldier ever did, it seemed, was to splash a bit of water on his hands and face.

So it was that Louis, who'd always washed from head to toe every morning, now had an odor he recognized all too well.

I smell like a white man.

He shook his head, thinking of the old joke among the Abenakis. No one ever needed eyes to find a town of the *Iglizmonak*, the English. Just follow your nose. White men never bathed. You could smell them from miles away. Now he had that same stink of sweat and dirt and other body odors about himself.

As he buttoned up his flannel sack coat, something stabbed at his right thigh.

"Ding dang and blast it!" Louis yelled, slapping his leg hard.

"That's the ticket, Chief, get them tigers!" Mickey Devlin trilled from the bunk to his left. Devlin's brogue, pug nose, and red hair marked him Irish for sure.

"Like many another sturdy son of the Shamrock," Devlin said when they first met, "enlisting in the army was me best bet for a job and a bit of respect."

Louis enjoyed hearing Devlin talk. His new friend's voice was so lilting that everything he said seemed like a melody, justifying his nickname of Songbird.

"Between eatin' with your mess mates and gettin' et by lice and fleas, we'll have you cussin' like a true son of the Fightin' Sixty-ninth before this war is over," Joker cracked, looking up from spitting on his shoes and wiping them with a cloth. "I overheard them bugs gettin' together and drawin' straws last night to decide who they was to eat first for breakfast."

And I was the short straw, Louis thought, squeezing the thick wool fabric between his fingers in the hopes of hearing the crunch of an insect's shell. As usual, his attacker escaped. One more tiger gone back into the jungle.

Tigers, graybacks, Rebels. Only a few of the words for the lice that were more numerous in their tents than enemies on the battlefield. Along with ticks, fleas, and chiggers, those biting nuisances had been waiting for them at Camp Meagher, drawn by the presence of so much easy prey. No matter how many you killed there were always two more to take their place.

What had Sergeant Flynn said about them? Sergeant Flynn, who seemed to know everything and was practically worshipped by Corporal Hayes, the broad-mustached noncom who followed him everywhere?

And no wonder. Their sergeant seemed more a force of nature

than a man. A lifetime soldier, First Sergeant Liam Michael Flynn was solid as a block of oak never sanded smooth. Thick, grizzled hair framed a wide bulldog face that looked to have absorbed more than a few blows—likely at the expense of any knuckles that hit him. He had a pugilist's stance and the heavy mitts to match, more like bear paws than hands. The deep voice that rumbled out of his chest made the air vibrate as if a bass drum had been struck.

"Lice?" Flynn boomed, when his recruits complained of being beset in their beds. "There's but three ways t' get rid of the wee beasties. First is by getting yerself a whole new uniform—which is impossible. Second's by bathing yerself and boiling your clothes—which is unlikely. Third's death—always a happy possibility."

Louis rubbed his leg, then fitted the slouch cap on his head. Their military hats were all one size, but since his head was one of the bigger ones, his bonnet fit snug and almost looked sharp. It didn't come down over his eyes like Merry's.

Not that Merry complained. Will Merry was almost as taciturn as Louis himself. The little recruit only uttered a few words now and then—in a gruff tone meant to cover up how high and boyish his normal voice was. But despite his shyness, Merry was the most helpful person in their company—even if he was also physically the weakest. Louis wondered if Merry had some sort of sickness like consumption that made him seem so frail. Though he didn't have the cough.

If he'd been looked at close, I doubt he would have gotten into this army.

Louis shook his head at the thought of the exam he and the others had gotten. The doctor had been more interested in the dime novel he was reading than the men brought before him in rapid succession. Every soldier was supposed to get a complete physical. For Louis and all the rest it checked just three things.

"Hold out your hands and take off your shoes."

To prove you've fingers enough to pull a trigger and two feet for marching.

"Stick out your tongue."

To make sure you can answer "Yes, sir."

Get tapped on your collarbone.

As to what purpose that tap served, Louis had no idea.

"Fit to serve. Next."

Louis made sure all four buttons of his sack coat were fastened, strapped on his belt, grabbed his musket, and scrambled out of the tent.

"Line up!"

And there they stood at attention, him and the nineteen other privates in his section in two ranks. Two corporals in front. Ready for the sergeant to call the roll.

The first day they'd tried it, they'd looked like a troop of clowns. The clumsy farm boy that Louis thought was named either Ike or Jake fell on his face as he tried to pull on the pants he'd been foolish enough to take off during the night. Kirk had but one shoe. Three of the others were without hats. Louis's coat was buttoned up wrong and Devlin had his musket upside down. Little Will Merry, who'd had the presence of mind to sleep fully clad, would have been the first to line up if he hadn't kept tripping on his pants legs.

Now, after two weeks of constant practice, their whole squad managed the lineup with ease. One after another, men responded smartly to the calling of their names by Corporal Hayes.

"Smith?"

"Here, sir!"

"O'Day?"

"Here, sir!"

And that's a wonder, Louis thought. Over the past week William O'Day had cut himself twice with his own bayonet, almost shot himself in the foot with his rifle, and stumbled at least twice over every stone on the drill field. *Bad Luck Bill.*

"Nolette?"

"Here, sir!"

"Wilson?"

"He-he-here, sir."

Shaky, indeed, Louis thought. That was the nickname the company had bestowed upon Kevin Wilson, a nervous, big-bellied Albany boy who often stammered. Joker was taking wagers on which man would be the first to run from battle. The only one with more bets on him than Shaky Wilson was . . .

"Belaney?"

"Here, sir."

Only the undertone of a sneer in his voice today.

"Kirk?"

"Here, sir!"

"Devlin?"

"Here, sir!"

"Dedham?"

There was a pause. Louis held his breath.

Jake Dedham was a rail-thin, good-natured farm boy. His lanky frame and the way his reddish blond hair stuck up at all angles from under his cap were the reasons the company settled his nickname the first day they were together.

"Scarecrow?" Jake had said with a grin. "Well, I guess that'll do."

Louis had never met anyone as pleased with everything around him.

"Soldierin'," Scarecrow said to Louis one day as they stood in the mess line, "is a sight easier than farmin'. I have took to it like a duck to a pond."

Day after day, though, at roll call Scarecrow persisted in raising a hand to the sky and declaring in a pleased voice, "Wull, that's me, for sure!"

He'd done so with such innocent eagerness that even Sergeant Flynn found it hard not to crack a smile. But it hadn't kept Flynn from taking corrective measures. Day after day Scarecrow was pulled out of his bunk early by their determined sergeant to practice the proper response.

Come on! Say it!

"Here, sir!" Scarecrow piped in.

Then, in a voice so soft that only Louis could hear it, Scarecrow added under his breath: "Me, for sure."

"All present and accounted for," Corporal Hayes concluded, turning toward Sergeant Flynn. "Even Belaney, sir."

Flynn nodded. "Corporal Hayes," he said in a gentle voice, "would ye be so kind as to run the lads through the drill our own beloved Brigadier General Silas Casey wrote down so well in his *Infantry Tactics*?"

"Yes, sir," Corporal Hayes replied, snapping a salute.

Louis had been taught by his father how to shoot a musket when he was six, but the army's detailed firing routine had been as foreign to him as the lilting Gaelic language the Irishmen of the brigade sometimes spoke to each other. Now, though, he knew the drill.

"Load!" Corporal Hayes barked, stepping to the side.

Louis stood his rifle barrel-up between his feet. His left hand held the muzzle eight inches from his body. His right hand reached into the cartridge box, its brass oval plate stamped *U.S.*, that hung from his belt.

"Handle cartridge!"

Louis pulled out a paper-wrapped .58-caliber cartridge and stuck the powder end between his teeth.

"Tear cartridge!"

Rip the paper from the end with my teeth. Spit the paper out. Bring the cartridge down in front of the muzzle.

"Charge cartridge!"

Empty the powder into the barrel. Disengage the minié ball from the paper with my right hand and the first two fingers of my left. Insert the ball, pointed side toward the sky, press it down with my right thumb.

"Draw rammer!"

Louis grasped the end of the rammer and pulled the long metal rod from its carrying groove by extending his arm. Keeping the back of his hand toward the front, Louis placed the head of the rammer on the minié ball.

"Ram cartridge!"

Louis pressed the ball home, remembering to hold his elbows near his body as he did so. There was a satisfying thunk as the minié ball seated itself against the black powder.

"Return rammer!"

Draw the rammer halfway out, Louis said to himself, his hands taking action before his thought. *Grasp it near the muzzle with my right hand. Extend my arm to clear the barrel. Turn it, insert it in the carrying groove. Force it home by placing the little finger of my right hand on its head.*

"Prime!"

With his left hand, Louis raised his rifle until his wrist was at eye level. He was standing half-face now, his right foot at a right angle to his left. He half cocked the hammer with the thumb of his right hand, reached without looking into the cap pouch at his side, pulled out a percussion cap, placed it on the nipple where the hammer would strike, pressed it down with his thumb.

"Shoulder!"

Louis swung the rifle to his right shoulder, feeling his heartbeat quicken a little as he did so.

"Ready!"

Check your foot stance, Louis reminded himself.

"Aim!"

Incline your head to the side to sight with your right eye, left eye closed. Look down the open V notch at the rear and center the blade sight. Finger on the trigger.

"Fire!"

Twenty .58-caliber Springfield Rifle Muskets belched out fire and clouds of white smoke.

Fifty yards away, a satisfying number of minié balls struck the barrel set up as a target, sending up a shower of splinters.

"Can I trust me own eyes?" Sergeant Fynn said, a disbelieving smile on his face. "Has someone gone and replaced me troop of city swells and country clodhoppers with what appears to be real soldiers?"

CHAPTER FIVE
MARCHING

Tuesday, May 3, 1864

Private Mickey Devlin was reciting poetry again.

"Now round the flag the Irish like a human rampart go," Songbird declaimed in perfect rhythm to their marching feet, "they found *Cead Mille failthe* here—they'll give it to the foe."

He looked at Louis, who nodded back at him. Even though he had no idea what under the sun that mouthful of words meant, they were stuck in Louis's own head now like a fly's feet in molasses.

"Devlin," Corporal Hayes said, stroking his thin red mustache with his thumb as he came up beside the Songbird, "those are fine enough lines. But you've been repeating them for the last five miles. Would you either favor us with something new or button your lip?"

"Forgive me, sir," Devlin replied. "It was just honor I was doing to the valor of our comrades, the living and the dear departed whose memories'll remain green in our souls as that same emerald flag under which they fought, the very flag that leads us now, proudly waving beside the starry banner."

"Aye, Devlin," Corporal Hayes sighed, "every man in the company knows you've kissed the Blarney Stone. Now find another verse or be quiet."

Louis, close behind Devlin in the line of march, shook his head. He'd met Irishmen before in the occasional jobs of labor that he had done. It was always the Irish, the blacks, and the Indians who were there in greater numbers to do such hard work. Though he'd stayed long enough to make friends with them, he never fully experienced just how much they loved to talk till now.

Of all the talkers and singers in the brigade, Devlin seemed the king. Louis had heard more speeches, poems, songs, exaggerations, and tales, more "blarney," from the stocky little Irishman in the last two weeks than from all the people put together in his entire previous fifteen years of life.

"We're the New York Sixty-ninth," Devlin warbled, making up a song of his own now from the way he paused between lines. "We fear no fight or foe." Then he grew quiet, perhaps to seek the next rhyme in his mind or because their line of march was now taking them up a steep hill.

The Fighting Irish 69th. Who would have thought an Indian boy like me could have become one of them? Yet here I am in a fine blue uniform and carrying a rifle and marching through northern Virginia.

The thought sent a shiver down his spine. He'd read in the newspapers about the Irish Brigade, the five regiments of which the 1,000 men of the New York 69th were a crucial part. At Antietam and Fred=ickburg, Chancellorsville and Gettysburg, men of the 69th had stood as firm as oak trees when others ran. They'd never retreated or lost a battle flag to the enemy.

If I'd been older I might have been with then. Back then there was real fighting going on and not just this marching back and forth to nowhere.

It was a week now since they'd left Camp Meagher. He was feeling what most of the other men in his company were—the nervous impatience of a young soldier not yet tested by battle. Then another, more sober voice spoke within him.

But if I had been old enough then, I might not be here now.

A year or two ago, as an Indian, he likely would not have been accepted into the Irish Brigade's ranks. At the start of the war, nine out of every ten men in the five gallant regiments had been born in Ireland. But, because of their bravery, no brigade had suffered greater losses. After Gettysburg, fewer than one man in four remained of those who had marched behind the green flag emblazoned with an Irish harp. To bring the brigade back up to strength, hundreds of men had been recruited with lightning speed. As before, most were from the working class, but now many were not Irish. There were Germans and Scots, French Canadians and even, like Louis, an Indian or two. The Union Army was no longer telling Indians who tried to sign up to go back home because this was a white man's war.

Though the Irish Brigade was less Irish in its makeup, the songs of Erin's Isle and the lilt of the Gaelic language were still everywhere—as was Irish nationalism. At times it seemed to Louis that the true enemy was not the South, but Great Britain, the pitiless nation that had turned the green soil of dear old Ireland into a desert and driven its finest sons into exile.

I may come out of this more Irish than Abenaki.

Then he shook his head, remembering the remark made to him that very morning by Joker Kirk.

"Chief, you haven't done a rain dance again, have you? We'd like to stay dry for once while we're marching."

The jest hadn't hurt his feelings, but it had reminded him yet again of who he was. His brown skin and Indian features would always make him stand apart from white men—even in this company of men who were becoming as close to him as brothers.

He didn't like being different. It made him feel less like a fighting man and more like a lonely boy.

Come on, Songbird, Louis thought.

It was better when Devlin was singing. It left less space in his head for him to think. But the hill was still steep and his red-haired friend clearly still cogitating.

He needed something to take his mind in another direction. Then he remembered something his father had told him.

"Do not just look at the world, my son, study its working. To know your way, see how things come together."

How things come together, that was it. Whether it was the building of a wigwam from bent saplings and bark or the makeup of an army, this Grand Army of the Potomac.

Ten men make a squad. Two squads make a section. Two sections make a platoon. Two platoons form a company, plus one captain, two lieutenants, five sergeants, eight corporals, and two musicians.

Company was about as far as most privates took it. Know your company and these three rules:

Stick with your company.

Follow your sergeant's orders.

If he goes down, listen to the corporal.

Louis, though, had learned more of the makeup of the army.

Ten companies made up a regiment. Five regiments make a brigade like our own led by Colonel Smyth. As brave a man as ever wore an officer's bars, Sergeant Flynn says. "Our colonel's words at the start of any fight will never be 'Up and at 'em,' but always 'Follow me, men.'"

Louis had seen Colonel Smyth just once, a big, broad-shouldered man with a thoughtful look to him. Mounted on a fine horse, he'd waved back at them all as he rode ahead of the line of march.

"Ye'll always see him like that riding in front of our own picket lines," Sergeant Flynn said. "It's a charmed life that fine brave man will have led if he comes out of this war alive."

They topped the hill now, went down the other side. As they trudged along, they passed a farmyard empty of all signs of life. Any livestock, from cattle on down to chickens, had "failed to give the password and suffered the penalty," as Joker put it. Every soldier welcomed a change from the salt pork and hardtack that made up most of their meals.

They were entering a cornfield now, further trampling down the already flattened grain. No rail fences standing to slow their progress. They'd been pulled down and chopped up as fuel for camp fires by the regiments that preceded them.

Regiments. Five regiments make a brigade. Two brigades make a division. Two divisions to a corps. Every corps has twenty-five cannons, fifty ambulances, two hundred supply wagons. Two corps make an army. And that adds up to . . .

Louis calculated in his head: *160,000 men or more.*

Going up an even steeper hill now, leaving the farmland behind. Aside from Louis, whose life on the road had accustomed him to walking great distances with a heavy pack on his back, most of the men were breathing hard. That was especially true of Bull Belaney, whose breath was coming in gasps that Louis could hear even though the suspected bounty jumper was a good hundred feet ahead of him. Bull had been placed in the first line of march by Sergeant Flynn.

"No straggling, skulking, or skedaddling for you, boy," Flynn had said when he caught Belaney trying to position himself at the back of the company.

Kirk caught his heel on a rock and almost stumbled. Louis reached out a hand to steady him without breaking stride.

"Thank ye!" Joker wheezed. "I take back what I said this morning. In this heat I'd be glad for a bit of rain."

One man farther over, Merry's round childish face was as red as a beet, but he was laboring on. The weight of packs, muskets, bayonets, and cartridge boxes filled with forty rounds of ammunition was over thirty pounds. Some of their company had started off with even more weight than that. Prized personal possessions had been stuffed into their packs along with blanket rolls, three days of rations, and full canteens. After the first five miles, the sun beating down upon them, the new recruits had started to jettison that extra weight. All sorts of things, from spare clothing, knives, and compasses to books lay on the hillside.

Something clanked under his foot. Louis looked down. It was a rounded plate of the sort some soldiers brought with them in the hopes that it might stop a minié ball.

Probably the same one that I saw Wilson tying over his belly this morning, Louis thought, kicking the abandoned piece of armor to the side. *Won't lay here long.*

Sutlers were close behind them. They hovered like the turkey buzzards, fellow scavengers following the army. Hated for their presence and missed in their absence, the sutlers offered such high-priced necessities as tinned meat, whiskey, tobacco, newspapers, shoelaces, candy, and playing cards. Always ready to make a quick profit, they'd swoop in to pick up any cast-off items and add them to the goods they'd sell.

Louis shifted his pack to swat at the air. His own load was five pounds heavier than most since he was carrying half of a shelter tent. He hardly noticed the weight, but couldn't ignore the gnats that formed a cloud around his face whenever he stopped walking for more than a heartbeat.

Downhill again, still not even the hint of a breeze. Hot as Hades, though it was only early May. Up north there might still be snow. But here roses as red as blood were in bloom by the roadsides.

Being so far south, we are closer to the land where summer lives.

There was a river ahead to cross. The name Louis had heard someone mention was something like the Rapid One. Most likely they'd just pitch their tents in the woods on the other side, set up camp, and go back into the endless, boring routine of bugle calls and drills.

"The Johnnies are beat," someone said from behind him in a rueful voice. Louis didn't look back. He recognized the voice as belonging to Happy Smith. Happy's nickname came from always being able to see the downside of every situation.

"Dang it all!" Happy groused. "Them graybacks'll give out complete afore we even get a chance to shoot off our guns."

A distant rumble came from ahead.

Thunder?

Louis listened close, trying to hear that sound again over the tromp, tromp, tromp of marching feet from his company and the hundreds of other men in front of them and behind.

44

Ten paces ahead, Devlin coughed to clear his throat, took a deep breath, and began to sing the words that had finally come to him.

> *"We've never swerved from our green old flag,*
> *Upborne o'er many a bloody plain;*
> *'Tis now a torn and tattered rag*
> *But we will bear it aloft again."*

Another rumble sounded again. Louder this time.

Not thunder, Louis thought.

CHAPTER SIX
SMOKE

Thursday, May 5, 1864

The crackling sound was coming from somewhere on the other side of the confusing tangle of hills and forests in which they'd found themselves lost. Rutted roads so narrow that they seemed no more than trails led off in every direction. Not a marker to be seen anywhere. Whatever signs there might have been had been taken down by the Southern soldiers whose land they were invading.

Sounds like corn popping, Louis thought, wiping the sweat from his brow with his sleeve. *But it's not. It's rifles.*

They'd advanced a mile or so since the battle began. It was nothing like what he had expected. Rather than ranks of Gray soldiers, all Louis had seen so far was tangles of cedars and vines, pines and heavy brush cut here and there by dirt trails and meandering streams. Midday sun hot on his shoulders. From the woods to his left came the familiar sound of a cardinal's song, *fweet-fweet-fweet, cheer, cheer, cheer.*

Louis sniffed the warm air. Smoke in it now for sure.

Somewhere ahead of them General Hancock, the Second Corps commander, had given the order to keep advancing. They'd find good ground ahead. At least that was what the colonel who brought back the order told them before he rode off.

Sergeant Flynn growled from the tree stump he was standing on to Louis's left, trying without success to see more than fifty feet up the twisted trail.

"Good ground for the Rebs, but not us. No way for the artillery to find them in these godforsaken woods. They'll be shooting at us from behind every tree. Babes in the wilderness 'tis what we are!"

Flynn was talking to himself in a low voice that he thought no one else could hear. He'd not yet learned just how sharp were the ears of the brown-skinned young man who made it a point to seem as if he were not listening.

The wilderness. A good name for where we are.

The sergeant hopped down from his perch. "Follow me, lads," he boomed. "Stick like a burr to the men to the left and the right of ye. If ye get confused, just march toward the sounds of the guns."

Louis cocked his head. Something was coming fast from up

ahead. Hoofbeats were thudding in their direction from one of those roads that disappeared into the woods.

"Cavalry," Louis yelled.

"Off the road!" Flynn bellowed.

The men of Company E scattered to every side. Hats and bedrolls went flying in their haste to avoid the hooves galloping down on them. Louis barely held on to his rifle as he dove and rolled, coming up against the sharp roots of a cedar that tore a hole in the right knee of his trousers.

As quickly as they had appeared, the company of Union cavalry-men was gone. They left behind a cloud of dust, the echo of hooves and jingling spurs, the memory of gaily decorated horses, shining boots, spotless blue uniforms, and plumed hats . . . and more than a few curses.

Louis rubbed his leg. It was bleeding just below his knee.

My first war wound. But there are no medals given for damage done by members of our own army—if the cavalry can be called that.

"And there go our thoughtful lads on their lovely great steeds," Sergeant Flynn called down from the top of the pine stump where he had taken refuge. "Bless their mounted souls—if they have any."

Louis understood the irony in Flynn's words. After only two weeks in uniform he shared the foot soldier's lack of affection for the danged horsey boys. Cavalrymen could dash in and out of battle as they pleased without even losing the crease in their pants. Their feet didn't burn from marching for hours without stopping or their backs ache from lugging a forty-pound pack. And every cavalryman seemed to take it for granted that the roads belonged to them. So what if they had to ride over a few common foot soldiers and make them eat mud?

Cavalry's job was to be the eyes of the army. Reconnoiter, report back on the strength of the enemy. But, after three years of war, the Union cavalry had earned the reputation of disappearing just when it was needed and then coming back with wrong estimates of the enemy's numbers.

Easier to hate the cavalry than the enemy. That was said by every infantryman from the lowest private on up to the top generals.

Joker limped up to lean on Louis's shoulder as he tried to dislodge the thorny branch wrapped around his ankle.

"Have you heard there's a reward being offered for dead cavalrymen, Chief?" Kirk said. "Five dollars if they're wearing gray and ten if they're in Union blue?"

Louis chuckled.

Joker poked him in the side. "Finally got you to crack a grin on that one."

Sergeant Flynn looked over the ranks of the company as the rest extricated themselves from the branches and brambles to re-form on the dirt track, three abreast. It took three men to pull out William O'Day, who'd once again justified his nickname of Bad Luck Bill by getting his foot jammed into a hollow tree.

Corporal Hayes counted heads. "Nineteen," he said.

"Belaney," Flynn barked at the man who was standing behind a tree to relieve himself. "Out and to the front. And don't let me be finding ye bending down to tie a shoe and let the line go past ye. I know every trick in the book of malingering, boyo."

Flynn turned and nodded to Louis. "Nolette, thank ye for yer warning. So now let's put ye to scout where ye can use those Indian eyes and ears of yers. Stay a hundred feet or so ahead and report back whenever ye see something."

The sergeant pointed up the road. "Unless our beloved cavalry comes back and tramples us all to death, we'll be meeting the enemy just beyond those hills. Now forward, march!"

CHAPTER SEVEN
STRANGE CONVERSATIONS

Friday, May 6, 1864

If the sun rose the next day, Louis hardly knew it. The morning brought only a thin haze of light to the smoky landscape he squinted at as he stood on the picket line. He wiped his reddened eyes with his pocket kerchief. It came away smeared with black. Some was from the ashes in the air. More was from the powder and smoke of his own gun.

Louis looked down at his weapon. *How many times have I fired it?*

He cradled the Springfield in the crook of his left arm and felt inside his cartridge box, counting with his fingers.

Six cartridges left out of forty.

Probably the same for the other men who'd survived the fighting. They'd need more ammunition from the supply train before the next advance. Though they could also forage for ammunition from the cartridge boxes of the dead. Whether Gray or Blue, it didn't matter. They all fired or were struck by the same .58-caliber rounds.

How many dead?

He shook out the kerchief and wiped his eyes again. They were watering something fierce. He wasn't crying. Or maybe he was. It was hard to be sure. Just as hard as it was to keep straight all that had happened in the last sixteen hours. It seemed more like a dream than anything real.

Who's still alive in E Company?

He looked over to his right. A slender figure barely visible in the mist and smoke raised a hand to him. Louis waved back.

Merry.

Merry, there on the picket line with him, had come through the fight unhurt. Maybe it was because he was so small. In the hail of bullets that struck all around them, not a one had touched him.

Louis had escaped injury too, though a crease across the face of the brass box plate on his cartridge box showed how close a minié ball had come to finding his flesh and bone. The impact had knocked him off his feet. For a time he wasn't sure if he was alive or dead. Then another soldier in blue with a blackened face grabbed him by the hand and pulled him up. It had to be Songbird, for he was reciting poetry.

"We miss full well a comrade's smile, the grasp of many a friendly hand," Devlin chanted. "Come on now, Nolette. 'Tis no time yet for a nap."

Devlin was alive too. But not Bad Luck Bill. O'Day's head had been broken open like a melon by a spinning piece of shell. Nor was it likely that Shaky Wilson was still breathing. The last he'd seen Wilson, he was leaning on a fallen tree and trying to hold in a red writhing mass spilling like snakes out of his belly.

Why is it that I see those men who've been killed so clear in my mind, but I can't recall who else among us isn't hurt?

It was strange. Even stranger that all through the confusion of gunshot and smoke, shouts and screams and the sounds of men calling for water or their mothers, not once had he seen the face of an enemy soldier.

One moment he'd been walking along, moving down the road that had become wider, though the surrounding woods were just as thick. Then he'd heard a sound from the forest. The cracking of twigs underfoot, the tinny sound of a canteen hitting a tree, the sound of a musket being cocked. No time to get back to the company just coming now around the bend. He took a deep breath, shouted.

"Ambush! Get down!!"

Then he was crouching down, crawling back to the company, the whole of the 69th under fierce fire from an enemy they couldn't see. What they shot back at were the flashes of flame from rifles thrust out from behind trees and rocks. Louis loaded and fired again, loaded and fired again.

"Follow me, lads," Sergeant Flynn's voice bellowed from somewhere in the smoke.

Some were dead or too injured to stand, but the rest of them rose up to follow the green flag of the Irish Brigade. Through the smoke and the mist, the only ray of light visible was that bright design of a sun bursting through the clouds above an Irish harp and the words *Faugh-a-Ballagh*. "Clear the way."

Clear the way.

Those words kept going through his mind as Louis ran and stumbled and fired, loaded and fired again at flashes of flame and gray shapes that wavered in and out of sight like ghosts.

Then they were in another clearing, this one littered with what looked like sticks bleached white by the sun. Until O'Day spoke the words that made them all look again at the scattered piles.

"There's dead men's bones all around us," Bad Luck Bill yelled—just before the shrapnel found his skull.

It was later that Louis learned how another terrible battle had been fought between Blue and Gray for the same wilderness a year ago. So bloody and brutal that the bodies of the dead were left unburied. As Louis pushed his way through the woods, he saw the ghastly remains of that struggle again and again. A rib. A long leg bone. A gap-toothed skull. Sometimes, next to those remnants of what had been a breathing human like himself, the rusted remains of a canteen, a bit of tattered cloth, the rotting bill of a cap too worn by the weather to say which side it was from. By the bank of a little creek, Louis came across skeletons of three horses half buried in sticky mud.

It was moist in the creek bottoms, but the rest of the land was as dry as those abandoned bones. So dusty dry that muzzle blasts from muskets began touching off fires. Artillery was coming into play now, the Union gunners shooting blind. Where shells struck, bigger blazes roared into infernos. Blue and Gray soldiers caught in the path were burned alive, especially the wounded as they tried to crawl to safety.

"Help," someone had called.

A hand reaching up from the smoke. Louis grabbed it, dragged the man from the blinding fire that crackled hot at their heels until they stumbled into one of the small streams that meandered through the thick forest.

The wounded man was stripped of his coat, had lost his pack and musket. Had his uniform been blue or gray? Half blinded by the smoke Louis couldn't tell, didn't want to know. He levered the wounded man up the bank without looking close, leaned him against a log. The man's hand reached up to grasp his shoulder.

"Thankee."

"Just stay down. You'll be safe here."

A familiar bellow.

"T' me, lads of E Company!"

Flynn and no other.

Louis followed the sergeant's voice up to the road where the tatters of their company were rallying behind the flag bearer.

Back again to shooting at muzzle flashes and phantoms.

Just think about the task at hand. Keep up a steady fire. Make sure you've actually pulled the trigger and that your gun has been fired.

Flynn had warned them about that during their first day of training, holding his rifle high in one hand and pointing at its barrel.

"Don't ye get so befuddled in battle that ye go ramming powder and ball into a loaded gun. Don't be one of them poor fools who do it not two or three, but as many as eight or ten times until they can no longer drive the ramrod in. Though they do keep trying."

Flick off the expended cap from the nipple before seating a new one. Raise the piece. Fire at any sight of a gray uniform. Fire at any flash of flame. Fire in the direction of those chilling Rebel yells that tell us to expect another onslaught.

Did any of his shots strike home? Likely not. Most shots fired in a fight went high. Some spend eight times an enemy soldier's weight in lead before they actually hit a man. Flynn had said that too.

The thrilling anticipation of his first battle, the wild excitement that surged through him when he fired his musket the first time were far behind him. As far behind as the eager boy going into battle he'd been.

Louis shook his head as he saw it again in his mind.

Men screaming from the woods where the fires were so

hot that pines exploded into flame. Johnnies, most likely. The shots aimed at them had been coming from that direction. He and the others in his company had to run like the devil as another blaze swirled down on them, a red whirlwind.

Exhausted by then. Dead tired even before the fight began after marching for seven hours. But they ran faster than any of them had ever run before. Death, hot as blue blazes, burned at their heels.

Then, somehow, it had been night. Louis had found himself sitting on the ground, leaning back against another man for support. Both of them too tired to turn around.

"Got any water?" the other soldier finally asked, voice cracking from dryness. "Lost me whole kit somewhere back dere."

Belaney, of all people.

"Here you go, Bull." Louis handed him his own half-filled canteen.

"T'ank you, me friend," Belaney replied gratefully before he drank. Not a trace of sarcasm in his weary voice.

Belaney.

That's who the other sentry was out there to his left. Belaney had been put on the picket line and stayed all night without trying to skedaddle. Silent and watching. He turned in Louis's direction as the smoke cleared.

Louis raised a hand. Bull nodded and waved back.

Now that Louis thought back on it, Belaney had actually

acted like a soldier all through the fight. At one point he'd even grabbed hold of the flagpole and held it aloft when the flag bearer had stumbled.

You never know what a man is made of until you put him to the test.

Like little Merry over there. Halfway through the night they'd exchanged a few words.

"You all right?" Merry had asked.

"Guess so," Louis had answered.

Then, out of nowhere, came the question that Louis had been asking himself.

"Why'd you join up?"

Wanting to show I could put on a uniform and prove myself as good as any white man? To get money to make life better for M'mere and me? Because I was a fool boy looking for excitement?

Too many answers to that question and no good one.

"Because," Louis answered and left it at that.

It hadn't deterred Merry from keeping on with the conversation, though. Merry reached for the gold ring on one of the fingers of his left hand. Louis had noticed that ring before because Merry was always doing that, touching it. A wedding ring most likely, though Merry looked too young to have a wife.

Merry caressed that ring as if it was giving some comfort in the dark, smoky night. When he spoke again, his voice was less gruff than usual.

"I joined up because my . . . my brother Tom was serving. I haven't seen him yet, but he's somewhere near here. He's a captain in the Sixty-third New York. He doesn't know what I did. I know he wouldn't approve. But I just had to try, because there might be a chance I could see his dear face and hear his voice. I even dream sometimes that because I'm a soldier I'll be able to save him."

Merry's voice broke and he stopped talking.

Louis said nothing in return, just reached over to pat Merry's thin shoulder before the two of them moved back to their posts. The little soldier had a great love for that brother of his. Louis respected that kind of family feeling.

Louis peered into the smoky haze that was passing for dawn. The hidden Reb pickets were close enough for him to hit them with a rock. But they weren't firing.

Being gentlemen this morning, giving everyone a chance to get breakfast, maybe, before we get back to trying to kill each other.

Louis was not guessing about how close the enemy was. The voice of that Southern soldier who'd spoken up sometime near midnight had been near enough for him to hear but his whisper.

It had happened just after Merry had wandered back to the farthest end of his part of the picket line.

"Yank, hey Yank," the man called to him in a whisper-soft voice.

It hadn't startled Louis. He'd sensed the presence of someone watching him for some time.

"Reb?" Louis answered in an equally low voice.

"Got any tobaccy?" the enemy soldier asked. A faint shadow

moved near the trees no more than ten yards away.

"Don't smoke," Louis replied, waited as the silence between them grew.

"Where y' from?" the man finally asked.

"Canada," Louis said. *No harm in such an answer.*

"Y' Indian?"

"Yup."

"Part Cherokee myself. From North Carolina. Just outside Raleigh. But I was a-working a farm here in 'Ginny when it started, so this is where I joined up."

"Unh-hunh," Louis said.

He could see the man's shape clearly now. He could bring his gun up and fire before this talkative Reb could take cover. But in his heart he knew that though this was the enemy, a soldier who might try to kill him the next day, it would be wrong.

"Awful ground to fight here, ain't it?"

The shadowy shape slid down to rest against the tree. What looked like a long stick was propped next to him. The man's rifle.

"Yup."

"That is why Marse Robert picked it, though. General Lee, he surely does know how to get advantage out of ground. Doesn't matter how bad outnumbered we might be if we kin jes' get the better ground to fight from. Second time we fought here, y'know. A year ago we whupped Hooker in this same wilderness. With the help of all them briars and grapevine and scrub, tanglefoot brush and snakes. Hooo-whee! Saw me a rattler must of been six foot long today. Then there's those fires. Sure would hate to get burnt up like some of our boys was today, wouldn't you?"

"Yup," Louis agreed.

A long silence followed. The man's shape seemed to melt into the dark. But Louis knew he wasn't gone.

"That there was my cousin you done pulled to safety today. Had you clean in my sights, but held off on shootin' when I seen what you was a-doin'."

"*Oliwni,*" Louis said. He didn't explain that it was the Abenaki word for thanks.

"*Wado,*" the man answered back in Cherokee.

Then it was almost totally quiet. Louis's keen ears, though, picked up the soft sound of someone slipping back into the trees.

"Indian?" the man said. His voice from farther away.

"Ay-yuh," Louis answered.

"I do hope you don't get kilt tomorrow."

"You too, Reb."

And that was the end of what Louis knew was one of the strangest conversations he'd ever have—even though it felt as if he'd been talking with a friend.

CHAPTER EIGHT
NEW WORDS

Saturday, May 7, 1864

The company's two drummers had survived the first days of battle. Bing and Bang, everyone called them, stocky twin brothers as alike as peas in a pod. Louis remembered how, four days before, the even ba-da-dum, ba-da-dum, ba-da-dum-dum-dum had stirred their hearts as they crossed the brown Rapidan River at Ely's Ford. Lee's army waited on the southern side of the Rapidan. The beat of those drums had kept feet together, minds focused on their march as the thousand men of the Sixty-ninth went into the Wilderness.

The work the regimental drummers were doing today, Louis saw, was different. No longer keeping feet together. They'd been assigned to the surgeon's tent behind the last line of field fortifications that had been hastily thrown up under the supervision of General Hancock's engineers.

The long wall of logs and soil stretched as far as Louis could see to either side. He stepped up onto the earthen platform that ran along the inner face of the parapet, shading his eyes against the glare of the sun with one hand.

Bing and Bang passed beneath him, carrying yet another wounded man into the blood-spattered canvas walls. Soon they'd be holding him down as the surgeon worked with scalpel and bone saw. They had a thing called chloroform, a liquid poured onto a cloth held over a man's mouth before they started the business.

Chloroform, Louis thought. *Another word I'd as soon not have learned.*

It knocked you out so that you never felt the pain. Louis was not so sure about that. Chloroformed or not, men still screamed and moaned as their limbs were lopped off like bloody tree branches.

Louis would have preferred to give the hospital a wider berth. But there was no other way to pass through to get his message back to the supply train. With a sigh he clambered down from the low breastworks and made his way past the tent. He was so close that he could hear Surgeon William O'Meagher's calm and polite voice addressed to the soldier who had just been carried in.

"Young man, 'tis sorry I am, but I must tell you straight," the sawbones was saying.

O'Meagher's voice had as strong an Irish lilt to it as any son of Erin in the brigade. According to Sergeant Flynn, O'Meagher had already been a doctor when he emigrated from Killenaule in County Tipperary. He'd served in the 37th New York at the start of the war, then re-enlisted as head surgeon of the 69th.

The tent flap was wide-open.

Don't peer inside, Louis said to himself.

But he couldn't keep from looking.

O'Meagher stood over the wooden table on which the wounded soldier had been placed. His hands were raised like those of a priest about to offer communion. But what he held was not wine or the Host. It was a surgeon's scalpel. Behind him stood Dr. Purcell, the assistant surgeon, holding a cloth and a bottle.

"The bone and flesh, you see, are mangled beyond repair," the gentleman surgeon explained to the soldier, whose eyes were closed tight, as if not seeing might prevent the loss of his ruined left leg.

"Remove it now below the knee, there are three chances in four that you shall survive." O'Meagher motioned for Purcell to step forward.

Like the man on the table, Louis turned his face away. He was sorry the moment he did. His gaze was now square upon what was behind the tent. It was evidence of how long O'Meagher and Purcell had been at work.

A grisly pile of arms and legs of men who might survive, but would never shoulder a musket or march again to battle lay stacked four feet high behind the operating area. If and when there was a lull in the action, those lost limbs would be buried in the same earth where men were digging trenches. No time for that now. Everyone in the tent, from the surgeons and doctors on down to the civilians who served as nurses, had too many wounded men to help.

Louis shuddered at the thought of being hit in his own arm or leg.

A minié ball catches a man in any extremity, the result's an awful mangling of flesh and shattering of bone. Struck square, there's little chance a limb can be saved.

He turned from the severed limbs toward the place where injured men were being tended by the volunteer nurses. One of them, a bearded man with a sensitive face, looked up toward Louis and nodded a greeting.

Louis nodded back. He'd seen the man before. His name, if he recalled it right, was Mr. Whitman.

Mr. Whitman turned his attention back to his charge, a stocky smooth-faced private who'd been struck in the knee and was waiting for the inevitable amputation.

"You did a fine thing," Mr. Whitman said as he stroked the lad's forehead. "It was brave of you to venture out as you did to bear your wounded sergeant back to the lines."

"Thank you, sir," the private said in a voice made tense by the pain.

"No," Whitman said, tears in his eyes. "No 'sir' to you, brave boy. Never sir. Just call me Walt."

Louis heaved a deep sigh and pressed on toward the supply depot.

Any fool believes war to be a grand and glorious thing, he thought, *let 'em spend a minute in the field hospital. War's a dirty business.*

A dirty business. When had he just heard someone say those words? It had been the morning before the battle, when they'd given way to let another brigade past. The bright banners and gaudy uniforms proclaimed it to be a Zouave Brigade, volunteers dressed like French Algerians in colorfully embroidered coats and tasseled caps. They cut a dashing figure in their perfectly tailored, scarlet-trimmed, dark blue outfits and red fezzes as they quick-stepped proudly by.

Corporal Hayes gave a low appreciative whistle. "The 140th New York," he said. "My Lord! They dress as well as they drill."

"Aye," Sergeant Flynn had replied, "and we'll see how they appear at the day's end. War's a dirty business and never ye forget that."

Dirty in more ways than one, Louis thought as he approached the supply train. Excavating soil was as much the business of a soldier as marching and shooting. *Digging trenches and graves. Scraping holes in the earth for the living and the dead.*

"Private Louis Nolette," he said, remembering to salute as he held out the folded piece of paper.

The supply sergeant, whose gray hair and pouched cheeks showed him to be a veteran of more than this conflict, took the message from him without bothering to open it.

"Would it be that you'd be wanting more shovels and cartridges, boy? Indeed, and I thought so. That's the need all up and down the line."

The old soldier looked toward the long line of supply wagons behind him. "It's well-prepared that we were for this—thanks to our good General Grant. Half of them wagons is filled with shovels and picks and the like. Enough for us to dig our way to China. And wouldn't we all rather be there now and not here?"

The old supply sergeant wiped his hands on his pants. "Isn't it a wonder how they always find some way to have us Micks digging ditches? That's what I was doing before I joined up meself. As sure as me name is Coyngham, I was one of them canal lads who finished shoveling Clinton's ditch all the way across the fair state of New York in October of 1825."

Louis nodded in understanding. His own father had worked for a time digging out the great Erie Canal.

Supply Sergeant Coyngham waved a hand toward the southwest.

"Now, the Rebels over there, they have another way of doing it. D'ye know that they have their slaves with them doing that hard labor of weaving those wicker baskets we call gabions and shoveling up the red earth into them to make their bomb-proof walls? They've pulled 'em from the plantations and the cotton fields to do all of the dirty work of war except for the actual killing. There's tens of thousands of 'em over there behind those lines. And there's a wee bit of irony. Here we are in this war that our wise abolitionists tell us is a struggle to free those poor benighted Negroes. And there they are over there sweating blood to build the fortifications to keep us out."

Coyngham shook his head. Then he clapped Louis on the shoulder. "But enough of me jabbering, lad. Go and tell your captain that supplies are on the way to the Sixty-ninth."

When Louis got back to the company there was barely time to eat a bit of the salt pork stew Merry had concocted over a campfire in the skillet that their mess shared. There were greens in it that actually added a surprising amount of flavor.

Though it might just be the hunger that has been eating at my belly so much that even an old shoe would have tasted good. I don't know which I worry about most—getting shot or not getting anything to eat!

Louis wolfed the final bite of his meager breakfast and washed it down with the last cup of coffee from the pot Merry had carried with him, tied with a spare shoelace to the back of his pack. Then he looked around at the other men in their mess.

Mess, another one of those new words I've learned. But now I take it for granted as much as breathing.

A mess was the smallest and the most informal of all the units in any army. And in some ways, Louis had learned, it was the most important, made up of those men who chose to take their meals together in the field.

They all shared the duties of cooking, cleaning up, fetching water to fill the canteens and the coffee pot, and—when they could pry it out of Merry's hands—carrying the iron skillet.

Joker Kirk and Scarecrow Dedham, Possum Page (flat on his back and snoring, his hat over his chubby face, able to take a nap anywhere), Merry, Happy Smith with his perennial scowl, Songbird Devlin, Knapp, Ryan, Kinney, Bishop. One by one he found the familiar faces of the other ten men in their mess. One apostle short of twelve, as Joker put it.

Not a one was missing. Men from other messes, like Wilson and O'Day, had died or become casualties. It was a small comfort that none of the men in their mess had been lost or even wounded in the hurly-burly of the previous day.

Every one of them, though, had broken fingernails and black, blistered hands. A stack of shovels lay piled against the side of their rifle pit. Their faces looked like those of the men Louis had seen once in a minstrel show, although the charcoal smears were not from burnt cork but from powder and ashes and Southern dirt.

And there—at the edge of the group—was one extra face. That face wore a look on it Louis had not seen before—a mix of uncertainty and hope.

"Belaney's asked to join us," Devlin said. "Every man in his mess was kilt or wounded. We've chosen to wait on a vote till you arrived. Ready? All in favor?"

It seemed Louis was not the only one who'd noticed how Bull Belaney had shown a new side to himself in the fight. Every man raised his hand. Even Possum, who woke up when the vote was called.

"Thank ye all," Bull said, his voice breaking. "T' explain

meself, you need t' know that I was sending ta money back t' my sick old mam in County Clare."

"Enough of that," Kirk said, "or you'll have us all crying in our beer. It seems that we're now the twelve apostles." He looked around the circle of unwashed faces with a grin. "And not a Judas among us."

"Or a Jonah," Happy Smith added with a growl. You could always trust him to think of the dark side of things.

A Jonah. Yet another new word I've learned.

A Jonah was sort of hapless soldier who seemed to bring misfortune with him wherever he went. A man who would catch his toe on a tree root and fall in such a way that half the company would trip over him. Lose his gun or his pack. Be the man whose shot went awry and hit one of his own. When they were to keep quiet and not alert the enemy to their presence, it was always a Jonah who would sneeze or cough. Like the cursed seafarer in the Bible, his fellows would welcome the chance to be rid of him.

Like poor O'Day, Louis thought. *And what would I do if bad luck should settle next on my own shoulders?*

"Form up on the double," a voice called from behind them. It was Sergeant Flynn. Behind Flynn were Bing and Bang, who'd been given yet another new duty. They were carrying a stretcher between them loaded with boxes of ammunition.

"Yer tea party is over, m'boys," the sergeant said. "Fill up yer cartridge boxes. See that yer well stocked with caps. When t'morrow comes it'll likely be up and advance."

But what the next days brought was more like up and down than advancing.

Shoot and shovel, Louis thought, wiping the dirt from his face and then raising his rifle. *Shovel and shoot.*

Work on their entrenchments, move a stone's throw forward and then dig again. Beyond their lines was a tangled landscape of brush and trees and smoke. The maze had been made even worse by fallen trees knocked down by minié balls that flew thick as swarms of giant bees. Some of those pines and cedars taken down neck high by countless .58-caliber rounds were as thick as a man's waist.

The Southern troops originally hadn't prepared entrenchments. They'd counted on their ambush working, the Northern army retreating in disarray. But the surprised Union soldiers hadn't given up or fallen back. Instead, they'd dug in.

Corporal Hayes came duckwalking down the trench, keeping his head low.

"No retreat!" he said, pausing by one man after another in the rifle trench, patting their shoulders, squeezing their arms. "Those were the orders sent down by Grant, and by the nails we're not about to go against them."

A hundred feet away the Rebs were digging in too now. Whenever he dared raise his head to look, Louis saw dirt flying into the air. They were piling more logs too. The barricade of logs piled breast high that was now a good three feet higher.

If there were military maneuvers going on, Louis was not

aware of them. Later reports might speak of how Hancock's gallant Second Corps engaged the Rebel corps of General Ambrose Powell Hill, how they drove the enemy back a mile and a half all through that day, holding off every attempt to outflank them or pierce their lines. But nothing as clear as that was what Louis experienced. It was just claw forward and dig in. Shovel and shoot.

CHAPTER NINE
FISHING

Monday, May 9, 1864

Late morning. The Wilderness was now three days and ten miles behind them—though it felt to Louis as if they'd marched a thousand. The road had been clogged with ambulances carrying the wounded in one direction, supply wagons creeping along in the other. The men of E Company had shuffled on through the night, never stopping to sleep, never moving faster than a snail's crawl. It had been more exhausting than striding forward at a brisk pace.

"What's holding us up?" Sergeant Flynn called out to a courier coming back from the head of the line of march. About two in the morning that had been.

"Cavalry," the man yelled. "Sheridan's on our side and Jeb Stuart's on theirs."

"Cavalry." Flynn sniffed. "I should have known."

It had taken till dawn for Sheridan's cavalry to move aside. The sun was coming up when they were told they'd reached their objective. No rest, though. Out with the shovels and up with the entrenchments. Shuffling forward and shoveling. Aside from drawing their rations, cleaning their guns, and praying for an hour or two of rest, that was about all they'd done for the last several days.

Louis took off his hat, but didn't peek up over the top of the trench. It was hardly worth the risk just to see a patchwork of woods and fields and low hills. Their objective, the Spotsylvania Court House and the crucial crossroads that led to the Rebels' main railway line, was a good five miles farther.

From where Louis knelt behind the walls of piled earth, the nearest Southern soldier might be half a mile or more away. But everyone in the army knew, especially after yesterday, how accurate the Southern snipers could be with their British Enfield rifles.

The Fourth and Fifth Corps, farther forward, had been led by Major General Sedgwick. "Uncle John," as everyone called him, was one of those rare, well-liked men who was also competent at his job. Grant always trusted his judgment. But yesterday, a clear bright Sunday, General Sedgwick's judgment had been less than perfect. As he inspected the forward line, he'd climbed up the entrenchment to look out on the field.

"Sir," an aide warned. "The Johnnies can see you there."

Sedgwick paid no attention, even though the bars on his shoulders marked him as an important target. Puffs of smoke appeared on the distant hill as Rebel snipers 800 yards away began to fire. The aide dropped to his belly.

"Why, what are you dodging for?" Sedgwick asked. "They could not hit an elephant at this distance."

Those were his final words. A Rebel ball struck the general square in the left cheek, killing him instantly.

Louis picked up the stick that he had found the day before. It looked as if someone might have been making it into a cane. He picked up his hat and balanced it on top of the stick. Then he raised it up above the top of the trench, counting under his breath in Abenaki.

"Nis, nas . . ."

Thwack! The stick was jolted out of his hand by the impact of the bullet. A second later he heard the distant pop from the gun half a mile away that had let loose that well-aimed shot. It proved what Corporal Hayes had said to him earlier that day, after telling him the story of Sedgwick's demise.

"When our boy Johnny Reb is that far away, you never hear the shot that kills you."

Louis picked up his hat. Untouched. The stick, though, had been split by the ball.

"Good on you, Nolette," Corporal Hayes said, patting Louis's shoulder as he shuffled up to him. "One less piece of Rebel lead to take the life of our boys."

Louis nodded. What he'd done hadn't just been idle play, but suggested to the men of Company E by their noncoms. Use your caps to fish for snipers.

Most, except for Possum Page, who had his slouch hat over his round-faced head and was snoring, were doing just that.

It was common knowledge that the Southern side was getting short of everything from men and horses to shoes and shot. Their factories had never been able to produce as much as the North. And the naval blockade was now keeping out just about all the supplies from England that the secessionists had been depending on. Whole companies of Rebel soldiers were said to be barefoot now.

Louis picked up the two pieces of the peeled tree limb that would never be a walking stick now. He didn't know what sort of tree it had come from. Trees were different here. But the stick had split clean down the middle along the grain, almost like ash wood.

You could make baskets from this, Louis thought, bending one of the pieces in his hand. He pushed that thought to the back of his mind. *No time for basket-making now or for thinking of my mother's voice calling me to come to the fire for supper.*

There was moisture in his eyes. He bent over to wipe them out. When he lifted his head again he saw Merry peering over at him. The tender expression on the little man's face made Louis think again of his mother.

How many times have I seen that same look of concern on M'mere's face?

A gentle, caring expression far out of place for where they were now.

"You all right, Louis?" Merry asked.

"Sweat," Louis said, wiping his cheeks again. "Hot today."

Merry nodded, but kept looking at him.

"Do you have a sweetheart?" Merry asked.

As soon as Merry asked that unexpected question the image of a certain girl came into Louis's mind. And even though he'd never thought of her as his sweetheart before, he almost said her name out loud. *Azonis.* But he didn't.

"Here," Louis said, holding up half of the stick and then tossing it over. "Try doing some fishing of your own."

Merry caught the stick and pulled off his hat. Merry's hair was chestnut brown and thick with curls. Its ends were as uneven as if it had been chopped off quick with scissors. Far different from Louis's own straight black hair, neatly cut at the nape of his neck.

"You need a better barber," Louis said, trying to make a joke.

"Pardon?" Merry said. "What did you say?"

"Nothing." Louis shook his head. "The Sixty-third isn't far from here. Maybe you'll see that brother of yours."

Merry's eyes lit up. "You really think so? I just long to see him, to . . . take him by the hand. That would be so wonderful."

"Might be," Louis replied. "There's always a chance."

CHAPTER TEN

ACROSS THE PO

Monday, May 9, 1864

"Lee's army now occupies a semicircular line three miles in length along this ridge here between the Po River and the Nye."

The lieutenant from the 155th knelt to draw with a stick on the earth. Louis wasn't quite sure of the man's name.

The lieutenant's words, of course, were not for common soldiers like him. They were directed at the officers and noncoms gathered in a tight circle to hear the order of battle. That they'd chosen to do this only fifty feet from Louis's position in the trench, though, meant that he was able to hear every word.

It helped that it was so quiet right now. There was just the occasional pop of a rifle now and then. With your eyes shut, you might forget for a moment where you were and imagine it to be a firecracker going off. Louis closed his eyes and listened. No firecrackers. But a mockingbird was singing from somewhere down in the brush that lay just beyond their trenches.

That bird, Louis thought, *will likely be glad once we've passed through. It's calm enough now. But the air feels like it does just before a big storm breaks.*

"The prisoners we've taken"—the young lieutenant dug his stick into the soft ground—"have told us that there are numerous weaknesses in that line. Especially this salient, here, near the center. Second Corps will advance to this side, occupy this small hill. Then we shall be able to enfilade the enemy's right."

He looked up from his rough map to smile enthusiastically at the intent circle of faces around him.

Louis scratched his stomach.

Louse or a flea this time? Could be either or both. Seems as if those two different sorts of critters have formed armies of their own along a line between my chest and my belly button. Us bugs propose to fight it out for control of this human's blood.

"Any questions?" Lieutenant O'Connell asked in a bright voice. Louis knew that was his name now. He'd just caught a glimpse of it on the piece of paper the young officer had pinned to his chest.

Lieutenant Michael O'Connell, Corcoran Legion, it read in a bold hand.

Just three days ago he would have wondered why a man would do a thing such as that. Now, though, he knew.

Print your name and your unit on a piece of paper and fasten it to your uniform. That way if you get killed, those who pick up your body'll know who you belonged to.

Louis rubbed his chest. He couldn't bring himself to pin a sign on himself that way. He hadn't even written the sort of letter a good many men always carried into battle in their pocket addressed *To My Dear Wife* or *For My Mother.*

"Well," Lieutenant O'Connell said again, "no questions?"

None at all.

Must be, Louis thought, *they know what* salient *and* enfilade *mean. Unlike me.* Louis leaned his back against the earth of the trench. *Then again,* he considered, *though I might not be able to parse out such fine military words, I know the meaning of it all. Tomorrow morning me and the others in Company E are getting sent out again to get shot at.*

He was only partially right. They didn't wait until the morning. Sergeant Flynn lined them up before nightfall. Corporal Hayes stood at his sergeant's left shoulder. As was always the case when Hayes was paying special attention and expecting every man to do the same, the corporal's right hand was on his chin, his thumb stroking his well-trimmed red mustache.

"Pack up yer gear, lads," Flynn said. "We're to take a bit of a walk in the dark. And, for the love of all the powers of heaven, be as silent as little mice. Nolette, seeing as how ye have the eyes and ears of an owl, ye'll be leading us out."

The sergeant paused to scratch his left forearm. Then he cursed and swatted his shoulder.

Fleas, Louis thought. *Lice don't move that fast.*

"And where might we be going, you ask? Well, we and the rest of the Irish Brigade will wade across the lovely river there," Flynn pointed, his index and middle finger held together like the barrel of a pistol, "and then make our way on up to that hilltop to the right of the bulge in the enemy lines. The whole of Second Corps behind us. Sure and if the luck of the Irish is with us, we'll have a few thousand rifles pouring lead into the Rebels from the side when the Sixth Corps attacks their middle at dawn."

The sergeant lifted up his beefy hand as if in benediction, though his sausagy fingers were quite unlike the delicate digits of the company chaplain. "Saints preserve ye."

Then he was off. Corporal Hayes nodded at them once, stroked his mustache, and followed Flynn.

Scarecrow Dedham took off his cap to scratch the straw yellow cowlick that always stood up like a rooster's comb when he was bareheaded.

"I swan. What'd all that mean?" the lanky farm boy said, a confused look on his face. Scarecrow was always the one who had the hardest time figuring out Flynn's flowery speeches.

"It means," Happy Smith growled, "we're going out to get our heads blown off in the dark."

Scarecrow grinned over at him. "You are a right caution,

Happy," he said, poking his friend in the ribs.

For some reason, though their personalities were like night and day, Dedham and Smith were almost always together now. Louis had no doubt that would be true tonight. Like David and Jonathan in the Bible, Scarecrow and Happy would be side by side, watching each other's back, even in the darkest dark.

And the night that settled in proved to be just that dark. No moon or stars could be seen, blocked out by the clouds that had begun gathering at dusk.

Rain coming, Louis thought.

Despite Flynn's admonition, the men around him were far from being as silent as mice as they climbed over the top of the trench. Brush cracked, boots thumped. All in all, though, they were quieter than Louis had expected. Every man had remembered to tie down his canteen and shovel and whatever else might clank or clatter as they made their way down to the river. And no voices were heard—aside from the occasional soft curse as a man banged against something or stumbled over a hesitant comrade's feet.

Can I do this? Louis thought. Then he remembered his father's words. *You climb a mountain one step at a time.* He nodded. *First step, find the river.* He began crawling forward.

It was no more than a hundred yards from their trench to the riverbank, but it seemed as if a hundred years passed before he smelled its warm waters and heard its rippling flow. He felt more than saw the shadowy shapes of the other men of his company close behind him. He reached back to pat the bony shoulder of Scarecrow, letting him know they'd reached their first objective, and should pass the signal back to Happy and from him to Merry and so on—a ripple of touch through their whole company.

Louis took a deep breath. *Can I do this?*

He wasn't afraid of what would happen to him. His deepest dread was that he would lead those other men, who'd placed their trust in him, the wrong way. He'd rather die than do that.

Nothing to do but go forward.

Lifting his rifle in both hands up above his chest, Louis swung his feet around and lowered them in. The water that rose around his ankles and filled his boots was almost as warm as blood. His feet didn't sink in so deeply that it mired him down, but the smell of rotting plants rose up as he waded deeper. Splashing sounds came from behind him. Hundreds of others were entering the river less quietly than he had. There was even the sound of what had to be someone falling in headfirst.

Too loud. Dang!

Louis gritted his teeth, waiting for the first volley of .58-caliber slugs to sweep through them like a scythe through grass. But no shouts or shots came from the Confederate lines that were surely only a few hundred feet from them. He reached back and tugged at the sleeve of whoever was behind him now.

Keep moving.

The water stayed shallow, no more than waist deep in the middle. Then only to his knees, to his ankles. Across the river now, moving up the bank in a crouch. Could he find the outline of the hill that was their objective? He looked up at the gray sky and then slowly down. There it was.

Keep a straight line. Just keep them going straight on.

He tugged again at the sleeve of the burly man in back of him now, who passed the signal to shadowed shapes of other men acting as scouts to either side just behind him. He shifted the rifle in his hands as he moved forward, a slow step at a time as the ground rose in front of him.

Minutes passed.

Or was it hours?

Finally, a lifetime later, Louis stopped.

We're on a hilltop. But is this the high ground we wanted?

A large hand grasped his shoulder from behind.

"Fine, lad," Flynn's voice whispered in his ear, "'tis the exact spot. Above and t' the right of their line. Now it's dig in and wait till dawn."

There was no way to hide the sound of shovels chunking down into soil and stone. But still, to Louis's amazement, no shots came their way.

Dig and keep digging. Every shovel full of earth may be one less bullet getting through to you.

His arms and his back ached, but he kept thrusting his short spade in to lever out more earth and gravel. At last he could dig no more.

Deep enough, Louis thought. He put down his spade. *I'll close my eyes for just a moment.*

When he opened them he saw three things.

The first was that the dawn light was breaking.

The second was a mockingbird. Was it that same one he'd heard singing until dusk the day before? The bird was perched on a little branch that hung no more than a hand's width from his nose. It cocked its head at him, then cheeped, spread its white-banded wings, and fluttered off down the hill.

As his eyes followed the bird's flight, Louis saw the third thing.

A chill went down his back. He understood why there'd been no response from the enemy to the sounds of their digging.

Those Rebs are so confident of their position, they didn't think it worth their while to waste lead in the darkness.

The fortifications below them were no simple rifle pits like the ones E Company had dug during the night. Rebel engineers had designed a massive earthwork, a great line of heavy logs backed up by tons of earth. Those fortress walls stretched for miles in both directions. Eight feet high with loopholes cut out near the bottom for riflemen to shoot from. And set back from that line Louis could see several gun batteries. Four twelve-pound Napoleons in each battery. When the battle began they'd be dropping four shells a minute on the heads of the attacking Sixth Corps.

The two thousand men of the Union's Second Corps might now be to the side and above this Rebel salient. But those Gray soldiers were so dug in you could hardly even get a sight of anything more than rifle barrels sticking out of loopholes.

We're to attack the middle of that?

Not only did the Rebs have that awe-inspiring fortification and all those cannons, but in front of the wall was a deep ditch backed by a fearful obstacle. Countless trees had been laid down side by side and staked in place, their branches sharpened so they stuck out like daggers.

If I'd led them wrong last night, we'd of blundered right into them pitchfork branches.

A shiver went down Louis's back

Any minute they'll be sending our boys to break that line. But how can any living thing bigger than a gnat get through?

CHAPTER ELEVEN
THROUGH THE RAIN

Thursday, May 12, 1864

"Seems to me," Devlin said, "that Chief here has granted your wish, Joker, me boy." He pushed up the rubber ground cloth that had been fastened to the headlog at the top of the parapet so that it formed a slanting roof over his part of the trench. The rain that had pooled on it ran down into the ditch next to him. "Ain't you going to thank him for this fine rain?"

"Rain?" Timmy Kirk said. "This is Noah's blessed flood. All I wanted was a few drops to cool my blistered feet. Possum, wouldn't you say Louis overdid it with his rain dance?"

Possum Page looked over, grinned, and nodded his round head.

Louis didn't say anything. It was just as he'd expected. He'd done nothing to encourage the rain pouring down from the sky with no sign of letup. He was not about to take credit for it, even jokingly. But if he denied it, the men with him might tease him even more or, worse, take it as a sign of modesty for his meteorological accomplishment.

Much as he felt bonded to the men around him, as close to brothers as any men he'd ever known, he found himself wishing again that there was another Indian he could talk to. Someone who understood what it was like to be such a figure of fascination or fun—sometimes both at once—in the eyes of his friends.

Because he was so quiet, his friends even seemed to think that nothing bothered him. They thought he was calm and didn't share their fears about failing or dying. Because he never cracked a joke back at them they thought he was serious and deep. Not just another boy who had no other choice but to pretend he was a man.

Louis wiped the rain off his face and readjusted his own ground cloth.

If another Indian was here with me now, I probably would still be getting teased by him about this rain being my fault. But it would be different because we'd both know that it wasn't.

He ducked out from under the cover of the ground cloth and stepped up onto the tread, the earthen shelf that raised a man high enough to peer through his rifle notch cut in the headlog.

"Any sign of anything out there?" Belaney said, leaning

over toward him. Just like all the others in the company, Bull assumed that Louis's eyes were better than anyone else's.

Just because I'm an Indian, Louis thought, *they think I can see more than they do*. Then he laughed at himself. *Well, as a matter of fact, I can.*

It was the simple truth. For whatever reason, Louis's eyes really were better than any of the others. But right now all he saw was that the steady shower had finally washed away the blood that had reddened the ground between the lines of Blue and Gray.

A full day had passed since the first Union assault on the U-shaped salient that jutted out of the Rebel lines like a mule's shoe. As planned, the men of Louis's company and the rest of Second Corps had laid down a steady enfilading fire from the right. Then the Sixth Corps had attacked head-on.

Cannons roared from both sides. Smoke obscured the battlefield. The Union artillery tore a hole through the abatis. *Abatis.* Another new word for Louis. It meant that deadly tangle of sharpened tree limbs set up in front of the Confederate line.

But the Reb cannons had been just as well-aimed. Shells poured down on the Union men as they tried to force their way through the breech. In the end, the fortified Gray line held. After a day of pitched battle, the Sixth fell back.

Now it was quiet. Maybe too quiet.

Louis wiped his eyes, shielding them from the rain with his hand as he tried to see a pattern of shapes back behind the salient.

Someone moved up onto the tread next to him.

"Something's missing," Louis said. A spyglass was placed in his hand.

"Use this, lad," Sergeant Flynn said.

Louis took the spyglass and raised up to get a better angle, leaning his elbows on the headlog. Clear weather, it would have been a risky thing to do, but the rain was like a curtain between them and the eyes of anyone who lacked Louis's keen eyes.

He scanned the slopes. Yesterday there'd been no fewer than five Rebel batteries of four guns there, each with the usual gun crew complement of dozens of officers and men for each field piece—officers, drivers, cannoneers. Twenty cannons roaring out their dragon's breath of fire and shot. But now there were none. Even the horses that pulled the batteries—six per gun and twice that number more to draw the battery wagon and the field forge—and the ordnance wagons of ammunition were nowhere in sight.

"The guns are gone, sir," Louis said.

"Excellent, me boy! Yer eagle eyes are a blessing to us." Sergeant Flynn slapped him on the back with such enthusiasm that Louis almost fell forward over the headlog.

"Corporal," Flynn called over his shoulder, "take the word back. It's just as we hoped. Dear old General Lee thinks we've given up here and called a retreat. He's moved his bleeding Napoleons to another part of the field."

Sergeant Flynn looked down from the tread at the men of

the company who had begun to assemble below.

"'Tis no time now for any fine, flowery speeches, lads. I'm not about to be like King Henry on Crispin's Day or to boast of what the Brigade did in years past when they broke the infantry of the Prince of Hesse and decided the fortune of the day. Nor will I remind you of the glory which the men before you achieved upon the plains of Ramillies, at the gate of Cremona, or on the plains of Fontenoy. I'll just point out to you that those examples of our Irish valor, regulated by discipline, are ones ye fine brave lads may at least try to imitate today."

Flynn paused to look at the rapt faces around him and nodded. "Sure and good men among us may go to a soldier's grave today," he said in a softer tone. "But we'll not let down the green flag nor the stars and stripes of this nation we've chosen to defend."

The sergeant stood up straighter and took off his cap in a wide gesture, ignoring the rain that ran down across his broad cheeks. "Our orders have been given to us. We're joining in the attack with the whole of the Second Corps."

Louis thought Flynn had forgotten he was standing next to him, but he was wrong. Flynn reached out an arm and wrapped it around Louis's shoulders in a hug so strong that Louis thought his ribs would crack.

"And thanks to the sharp eyes of me lad Private Nolette, I've some good news for ye all. The Rebels below us have drawn back their cannons, so there'll be no artillery pounding us as we head into the fray!"

"Huzzah!" someone shouted from the group of men below. It was Scarecrow, of course. When it came to eagerness, he always took the cake. But his cheer was quickly echoed by the whole group.

Have they forgotten, Louis thought, *that there's still a thousand or more Rebs with rifles down there?*

But he too felt the excitement that was sweeping through them, saw the light in the eyes of Corporal Hayes as he stroked his thin red mustache.

This time, this time we might break through.

Flynn turned, letting go his grip on Louis's shoulders, and pointed down.

"Twenty thousand men will be joining us, me boys. We are going to take that Bloody Angle down there. Our own brave General Hancock is leading the main force that will be striking this very dawn."

Flynn paused, then raised both hands toward the rainy sky.

"God willing," the sergeant said, his voice growing louder, "the enemy won't know what's hit them till it's too late. Now shoulder your arms and make ready! For when the shots and shouts rise to tell us the battle's begun, it's up and over the top again for us all."

CHAPTER TWELVE

THE MULE SHOE AND THE BONNIE BLUE FLAG

Thursday, May 12, 1864

Louis listened. He was soaking wet, the water dripping off his cap as he leaned forward. He no longer had his rubber blanket over his head, nor did any of the other men in the company. They had taken them down, rolled them, and tied them to their packs. They'd soon enough be leaving this trench. Once they went over the parapet there'd be no chance of coming back to claim any possessions left behind.

Possum Page was at Louis's left, his head nodding up and down.

"Hey Chief?" Possum whispered.

"Yup," Louis said.

"Could you pinch me and wake me if you see I've gone and fell asleep?"

Louis turned and stared.

"What?"

Possum nodded his round head even harder. "I cain't help it," he said. "When I get scared, all I want to do is just close my eyes and pretend it's all just a dream. But I guess it doesn't do much good 'cuz when I wake up I'm still here. I'm not back home with my ma and pa and my two little sisters. Y'know, I never got further than five miles away from home afore. I just miss them all dreadful much."

Louis reached over and put his hand on Possum's quivering shoulder.

"All right," he replied. "I'll do just that."

"I'm not like you," Possum said, his voice low and intense. "Seems there's nothing can scare you. I guess you got spirits or something that is protecting you. Could you maybe talk some more with me when this fight is over? I'm thinking that it might help me some. I'd like not to be afraid so much."

It was the longest speech he'd ever heard Possum make. It made Louis realize that, in a way, Possum was like himself, a scared boy whose friends didn't see what was going on inside him. To them he was just Possum, who could sleep through the Final Judgment.

Louis turned toward Possum, reached out and grasped his right hand. "Shake on it," Louis said. "We'll talk after the battle's over."

Possum grinned. His shoulders relaxed and he let out a deep breath.

Somehow, Louis thought, *those few words I just said meant something to him.*

"I sure do appreciate that, Chief."

Louis let go of Possum's hand and cocked his head.

What was that soft thumping noise? Even through the rain Louis began to hear a muffled sound with a familiar rhythm to it. It came from off to their left.

Louder now.

Thump-thump.

Thump-thump.

Thump-thump.

Thump-thump.

I know what that is. Even wet earth could not hide the metronomic thud of thousands of feet of men in blue approaching across the rain-curtained land.

Hancock for sure, his whole corps trying to march silent.

But even with no sound of drums to keep them in step they'd fallen into step. No enemy ears seemed to have noticed their approach, even though the surface of the water in the rain puddle at his feet was now quivering in time to the thuds. Soon they'd be right on top of the Rebel pickets watching halfheartedly for a Yankee attack they doubted would come.

In all the battles before this, that had been the Union pattern—fall back if the first hard assault fails. Lee and his boys hadn't learned yet that General Grant was not one to turn tail. He had sent orders all the way down the chain of command that they were to fight it out on this line even if it took all summer.

"Hear that?" Louis whispered to the man who'd come up on his right in the half darkness.

"Hear what?" Merry said.

Louis shook his head. He wasn't sure. It might have been the muffled sounds of a Confederate sentry being overpowered—his mouth stopped by a hand clamped over it or the thrust of a bayonet. Desperate deeds were being done down there under the cloak of the pouring rain.

Louis found himself thinking, as he always did now before fighting began, about the men on the other side. Louis hadn't been able to stop such thoughts since that night when the Rebel sentry spoke to him out of the darkness.

"Do you find it hard to hate them, Louis?" Merry asked.

It surprised Louis how close that question was to what he'd been thinking.

"I do," he answered.

"I too find it very difficult," Merry said. "But the thought that one of them might kill my . . . my brother makes me determined to stand against them. If my Tom should fall to Rebel guns I would hate them. I would hate the South forever."

Louis started to reply that he understood. But his words went unspoken as what had first started as a single shout from a Union soldier was taken up by one man after another until it became a great cheer. Thousands of voices lifted from below as Hancock's men, having overpowered the sentries, reached that jutting salient, and poured through the Mule Shoe.

Who was it who then shouted the order for E Company to stand, climb over their own parapets, and charge down into the fight below?

Corporal Hayes? Sergeant Flynn? Young Lieutenant Finley waving his sword? Or was it all of them at once?

In the sound of the shouting, the steady wash of the rain, and the pounding of his own heart, Louis could not remember. All he knew was that he and the others had taken up that cry and were running headlong downhill.

The Rebels were so taken by surprise that almost no shots were fired. Sixth and Second Corps split the Rebel line like twin bolts of blue lightning. Men in gray grounded their weapons and raised their hands. In the time it took a man to have breakfast, they took not just the position, but captured three Confederate generals and 4,000 men. They even caught up to the artillery train and took possession of those twenty cannons being moved down the line.

Louis stood with a smiling group of the men from E Company on a hill in the midst of a stand of pines. They could hardly believe the victory they seemed to have won. Even the rain had let up. The sun was about to break through the clouds.

"Whooo-heee!" Possum Page yelled. "Them Rebs is running all the way back to Richmond. This is how war ought to be fought, Chief! We'll be home by the Fourth of July!"

He started to do a little jig, raising his rifle over his head. Then, for some reason, he threw his rifle away.

As it spun past Louis's head, he saw that the butt of the Springfield was broken and splintered. A red stain was spreading across the middle of Possum's back. The young soldier who'd been able to sleep anywhere turned slowly, then crumpled like a doll made of rags into his final rest.

Minié balls were whizzing past them now from both left and right, peeling the bark off the pines.

Twenty feet ahead, Happy Smith and Scarecrow Dedham stood as if their feet were stuck in tar. Puffs of dust burst from their clothes as balls struck, holding them up for a terrible breathless moment before their legs gave way and they dropped to their knees.

"Get down for the luv of Mary!" Devlin shouted in a voice that was half a sob. He yanked Louis's belt. *"Down!"*

Then they were on their knees and stomachs, crawling backward, firing their rifles, rolling over onto their backs to reload, firing again along with the hundreds of other retreating Union men around them caught in the counterattack. A whole division was coming at them.

Midnight. No more sounds of gunshots or shouts of officers trying to rally their men. As close to quiet as it had been since the start of the dawn assault that had seemed destined to take them all the way to Richmond before the 10,000 men of General Gordon's Rebel reserves struck back. The exhausted stillness of the night was broken now only by the moans of the wounded who lay in the field between the lines of the two opposing armies.

Louis sagged against the back wall of the rifle trench and looked first to one side and then the other. No one from E Company to be seen. In the desperate confusion of the fight, Second Corps had been torn asunder. What remained was a mix of companies and regiments stitched together like patches in a quilt.

At midday, in the mad back and forth of attack and counter-attack, Louis had found himself in the midst of this squad of Corcoran lads from the 155th New York. The officer in charge was none other than that same Lieutenant Michael O'Connell who'd told them three days ago that they would be crossing the river. Three days? It felt as if three years had passed.

"It's the heart of the secession we're facing," Lieutenant O'Connell shouted as Louis joined the squad that was pushing back a larger force of Confederates.

Second North Carolina. That was what the enemy flags read.

O'Connell pulled off his hat and waved it over his head. "Pour it into them, boys! Break them and we've won the day. Drive those Tarheels back!"

That was when the Rebel general came at them atop a great black stallion, galloping out of the smoke and the mud as sudden as a ghost. Louis, who'd been standing by the lieutenant's side reloading, fell backward as the horse slammed into their line while the Gray officer on its back fired shot after shot from his .36 Colt Navy revolver into the mass of Union men around him.

The horse reared over Louis as he lay on his back.

Have I managed to finish the sequence of loading? No time to check. Pull the trigger!

Fire belched out of its barrel as his gun kicked hard against his shoulder. The Confederate general's arm jerked back as if struck by a club. The Navy Colt spun free to land in Louis's lap.

"Thuh gennul's down," a Rebel soldier screamed.

"Rally to General Ramseur," a bearded officer in gray shouted.

The Rebel general stumbled to his feet, clasping his arm. Before any Union soldiers could take him captive or get off another shot, he was surrounded and pulled back by his men.

Louis used his musket like a cane to rise to his feet. His left arm was bleeding. He remembered seeing a bayonet coming his way, slicing into his sleeve. He felt his forearm.

Cut, but not too deep.

It was worse on his other side. His right shoulder ached from the kick of his own rifle. He looked down at the handgun he'd grabbed as it landed in his lap.

Not the kind of gun a private ought to be carrying.

"Sir," he said, turning toward the place where Lieutenant O'Connell had been standing. "You want this?"

The lieutenant wasn't there. Louis tried to wipe the grime from his eyes. He was half deaf from the sounds of so many muskets going off near his ringing ears.

"Lieutenant?"

Lieutenant O'Connell lay on the ground. His hand still clutched the hat he'd been waving to rally the men. His eyes were wide-open to the sky, but they saw nothing in this world anymore.

Then Louis heard the singing.

"We are a band of brothers . . ." rang from somewhere in the retreating mass of enemy soldiers. It was a voice as clear and true as Songbird Devlin's, but its accent was that of the South and not Tipperary.

For a heartbeat it seemed as if every other sound on the battlefield stopped. Blue and Gray alike harkened to the painfully sweet melody.

> "We are a band of brothers,
> and native to the soil,
> Fighting for the property
> we gained by honest toil;
> And when our rights were threatened,
> the cry rose near and far,
> Hurrah for the Bonnie Blue Flag
> that bears a Single Star."

Then that voice was no longer alone. A hundred, a thousand, and two thousand more Rebel soldiers joined in the chorus.

> "Hurrah! Hurrah! For Southern Rights Hurrah!
> Hurrah for the Bonnie Blue Flag that bears a Single Star."

As lovely as that melody was, it was deadly as shot and shell.

It rallied the nearly beaten men out of retreat. Shouting that anthem of Southern patriotism, defiant against all invaders, the inspired Rebels began to advance. The Union soldiers fell back before the terrible beauty of a song.

Louis rubbed at his left hand. *Why is this bothering me?* He turned his hand up to look. His palm was black and blistered.

If M'mere were here, he thought, *she'd make me a poultice for this. Or she'd just pluck some wide hairy leaf, like from a bandage plant—mullein. The one some call flannel leaf. Then she would have me walk around all day with it clasped in my hand. And by the time night came, the leaf would be almost gone and my hand would be well.*

No matter what it was, whether a fever or a cut or a sick stomach, his mother always knew the remedy. Not one from a box or a bottle, but from the medicine plants themselves. M'mere. He closed his eyes, trying to find her in his memory. And there she was. He saw M'mere as clearly as if she were there beside him. Her back to him, her medicine bag slung over her shoulder, she was kneeling to speak words of thanks to a large-leafed plant. It wasn't one that Louis remembered seeing before, though it did look a bit like mullein. But the leaves were darker green and there was a fuzzy blue flower at the end of a leafy stalk. His mother pulled free a large leaf from the base and turned toward Louis, smiling as she held it out to him. He lifted his hurt hand. Then the throb of pain from his palm made him blink.

And in that blink of an eye the vision of his mother vanished. Louis found himself back looking at his injured palm.

When did I get this burn?

As soon as he mouthed those words he remembered. The Confederates had only been able to push them back to the other side of the entrenchments. There the advance had stalled, but the fighting had not. Divided by only a single rampart, Blue and Gray struggled back and forth. More Union troops tried to push into the gap. But they were packed too close. No one could get through. Men screamed as they fell and were trampled into the bloody red muck by the milling mass of soldiers trying to push forward. Among them, Louis remembered seeing the faces of their two drummers, Bing and Bang. Boys whose real names he'd never known, disappearing under the boots and bodies. He tried to reach out toward them, but it was no use. They were lost in the tangle of legs. Then, in the midst of that madness, Rebel gun barrels began to bristle through every loophole in the breastworks to explode at point-blank range.

Louis nodded. *That was when.*

A rifle had been thrust through at his face. To save himself, he'd grabbed the barrel, pushed it up and away. Near red-hot from firing again and again, the steel had burned his palm, but the ball had missed him—though the blast made his head ring as if he'd been swatted by a giant. As that empty rifle pulled back, he raised his own Springfield and fired it through the same notch in the headlog.

"Keep it up," an officer next to him shouted. "We're bringing up more ammunition. Hold the line."

By the side of men whose names he would likely never learn, shooting at enemies whose faces could not be seen, Louis reloaded and fired.

And held.

At last, deep into the night, a bugle sounded from the other side of the embattled line. Those Gray soldiers who could still stand, walk, or crawl fell back, dragging wounded and dead, fading into the darkness.

Days later, Louis read a newspaper account of the battle. They called it the Bloody Angle. The cost to both sides was 12,000 men.

Louis's mind and heart ached as he tried not to remember the song that had stirred those Gray soldiers to such fearful bravery. But it kept going through his head. Perhaps it would be there for the rest of his life, that bittersweet melody about a bonnie blue bloody flag.

CHAPTER THIRTEEN
MAIL

Saturday, May 14, 1864

"Dedham?"

No answer.

"Smith?"

No answer.

"Page?"

Silence again, Louis thought.

Sergeant Flynn, a bandage around his left arm that matched the one on Louis's right, stood alone as he called out the names. Both of his corporals were among the missing. Along with their two noncoms, half of E Company failed to answer. Killed like Possum and Happy and Scarecrow or so gravely wounded they'd never fight again. Like Knapp and Kinney and Bishop—the three of them minus enough arms and legs between them to fill another man's complement of limbs. Or missing like Corporal Hayes and Ryan, lost in the mud and the mist. Dead, dying, being held prisoner? No one knew for sure.

Who's left? Just me, Sergeant Flynn, Bull, Songbird, Joker, and . . .

"Merry?

"Here, sir!"

His small friend with the face of a child had proven tougher than many soldiers twice his size.

Sergeant Flynn paused at the end of the roll. He looked slowly at each and every face.

"Me boys," Flynn began. Then he let his hands fall to his sides. "I've no fine words for ye. Jes' take some time t' yourselves while ye can."

They looked at one another as Flynn walked slowly away. Then Merry wandered off, leaving just the four of them sitting there. Devlin, Belaney, Kirk, Nolette.

Devlin cleared his throat. *Was he going to raise a song?*

Instead, Songbird pulled a deck out of his pack. "Cards?"

There was a long, tired silence. Then Joker sighed.

"Poker. Sounds good to me about now. Especially when the joker's wild. How about you, Bull?"

"Arrh," Belaney replied, "poker's ta game me pa told me to fear like ta devil. But after ta last few days, the devil seems tame t' me. Deal me in!"

106

The three of them turned to look at Louis.

"Come on, Louis," Songbird said. "Naught to lose but the pay we've yet to see."

"More fun than a toothache," Belaney added.

"Yeah, Louis." Kirk nodded. "Play a hand or two with yer mates."

My mates, Louis thought. He took in each of their faces. Mates, indeed. Brothers despite the fact that he was Indian and they were not.

I'd give my life in a fight for any one of them. And I'm not about to let them see me cry. And just now not a one of them called me Chief.

He raised up his hand. "Maybe later," he said, standing and walking away before they saw the tears in his eyes. He wasn't sure where he was headed. But then someone called from farther down the trench.

"Louis, Louis!" It was Merry beckoning to him, pointing.

A covered wagon was pulled up on the small dirt track behind their trench.

"Come on," Merry said, tugging at Louis's sleeve. "There might be a letter for you from your mother!"

His small friend was smiling as he hurried toward the horse-drawn covered wagon with the letters *U.S. Mail 2nd Corps* printed large on the canvas.

The first smile I've seen in days.

The day before Louis had come upon a man from the 28th Massachusetts sitting next to his best friend's body in a ditch, cap in hand. Every now and then he would turn his head up toward the sky and laugh out loud. But there was no joy in that bitter laughter.

Merry, though, was pleased to the point of being giddy.

How can anyone smile now?

Louis stopped to kick mud from the soles of his boots.

But who am I to judge? I hardly know how I feel these days from one moment to the next, unless it's just plain confused. And maybe there is mail for me from M'mere.

The thought of mail or even a package from home could bring a smile to many a soldier's face. Despite the dangers and difficulties of war, nothing seemed to stop the weekly arrival of the mail. Even the gumbo of the Virginia roads that bogged down most other freight had not been able to prevent the arrival of the lighter mail wagon pulled by two big draft horses. It was even more welcome than the paymaster—who had yet to show up during the month and a half Louis had been in the army.

Six weeks. Is that all?

Yet he felt at times as if he'd been a soldier forever, wearing itchy and ill-fitting clothing, scratching at fleas and lice, almost breaking his teeth on the so-called bread that was hard enough to put a dent in a man's skull. One joke running through Second Corps was that by the evening of the fight at the Bloody Angle, Company C had run out of ammunition. So they'd started hurling hardtack and the enemy had panicked and run.

Other times, though, other times I can't believe I'm here.

Just two nights before the battle he'd woken up in confusion. Where was he? Out in the little camp in the woods where he went to cut the trees to make their baskets?

Toni, nigawes? *Where are you, my mother?*

Gradually, it came to him. He was farther than the other side of the moon from the poor but peaceful life he had known.

Writing or receiving letters were his only real connections to that distant life an innocent boy had once lived. That was why he wrote so regularly to his mother, even though stamps, which didn't have any weight to them like a coin, cost a dime. He passed up sweets from the sutlers' wagons to buy those little pieces of paper that would insure his words got carried safe to his dear mama.

He'd received just one letter thus far from M'mere. The wording was clearly hers:

Your Mama, she does miss you, my son.
I pray Bon Dieu that you be well.
I am glad you wrote to me and that you
are alive.
Your Mama, she sends you all her love.
I sign this letter now.
                    Your Mama,
                        Sophie

But the writing in pen with florid curlicues was nothing like the laborious printing that marked his mother's hand. She must have paid someone to take down the words as she spoke them.

Simple as those words were, Louis read a whole world of meaning into them. He carried her letter in the pocket closest to his heart.

Mail. Is that why Merry is so happy today? Does he think he's going to get mail? Louis shook his head. *That can't be it. Didn't Merry tell me that he enlisted in secret? No one in his family, especially not his brother, knows where he is.*

Suddenly Louis knew. He grabbed his friend's thin shoulder, spinning him around.

"You saw your brother!"

Merry danced away from Louis's grasp. His face was now bright with excitement.

"Yes," Merry said. "Oh yes! In the afternoon, during the battle, I was no further from him than I am from you. And Louis, it was like my dream. I protected him. I shot my musket at an enemy soldier who was taking a bead on him. I don't know if I hit him or not, but the man was gone after the smoke cleared, and Tom was safe. And Tom knew I'd done it. He turned right to me and thanked me for saving his life."

"Was he angry because you were there?"

Merry blushed. "He didn't recognize me. How could he? I mean . . . he'd never seen me before in a uniform. My face was black and dirty. I didn't say anything for fear he'd know my voice. If he'd known who I was he would have tried to protect me and risk his own life. When the fight was done, I made my way back here to our company."

Merry's voice choked. He grabbed Louis's sleeve again and tugged hard at it. "Do you understand?"

Louis wasn't sure that he did. But he nodded his head anyway.

The two of them had reached the mail wagon. As always, Louis went first to the horses. Others tried to shove into line to ask if there was anything for them or to be close enough to reach out right away if their name was read off of a letter or package. But not Louis.

At least one man ought to let these horses what have worked so hard know they are appreciated.

He ran his hand along the neck of the big white mare on the right.

"You're a fine faithful girl," he said as the horse lowered its head toward him.

Merry, who'd been at his side, suddenly choked back a sob. The little private walked swiftly away, wiping his face with his sleeve.

CHAPTER FOURTEEN

ANOTHER INDIAN

Sunday, May 15, 1864

The Lord's Day seemed to make little difference to those who were running the war. One day for killing was the same as the next. This Sunday, though, seemed destined to be a quiet one.

We're both worn out, Louis thought. *Blue and Gray alike.*

Morning services had ended no more than an hour ago, but he couldn't recall a word the chaplain spoke. He raised his face up to the noon sun, shining down brightly for a change.

Be thankful, he thought. The old words his father taught him came back to his mind.

Ktsi Kisos, okeohneh. Great Sun, thank you for shining down on me.

May, but warm as a summer day in August back north. If

it weren't for the throbbing in his burnt hand, he might have been able to imagine himself back there.

"Louis!"

"Chief!"

Louis sighed and opened his eyes. He wasn't surprised. He'd heard the feet of people coming his way across the field.

Joker, Songbird, Bull. Merry too. But, to his surprise, someone else was with them.

"Look who we've brung ye," Songbird said, gesturing forward the stranger standing behind them.

"One a' yer own," Belaney said, an unaccustomed smile on his dark face.

"We got you a red brother!" Joker grinned.

Louis had never seen the Union soldier who stepped forward before. The young man's skin, though, was the same brown as his. His eyes were as dark, his hair as thick and raven black. He was shorter and stockier than Louis, but he carried himself the way one does when years of outdoor living have made you as graceful and strong as a wolf. There was a little twist to his lip, a half smile there as his eyes took Louis in.

"*Sehkon,*" the other Indian said in Mohawk, a language Louis recognized, even if he didn't speak much of it.

Great, he thought. *They have brought me an Iroquois!*

Louis rose to his feet and raised a hand in ironic greeting. "*Kwai kwai, Maguak,*" he replied.

The half smile on the other young man's face twisted a little farther.

"Abernaki, eh?" he said.

"Un-hunh," Louis replied, taking a stiff-legged half step forward.

"Adirondack is what we call you. Porcupines, Bark-eaters," the Mohawk soldier said, taking his own stiff step, the two of them almost chest to chest now.

By now, Louis's friends from E Company were exchanging worried glances. This wasn't going like they'd expected.

Louis thrust his chin forward. "Maguak, we call you. Those afraid to fight us."

"Friend of those French pigs who burned our fields!"

"Ally of those English dogs who destroyed our villages!"

Out of the corner of his eye Louis could see that Joker was standing with his mouth wide open. Songbird looked stricken, Belaney shocked, and Merry seemed about ready to cry.

"Enemy of my friends," Louis growled.

"Friend of my enemies," the Mohawk soldier hissed back.

"Now we must fight each other," Louis said, bumping his chest against the other man's.

"A struggle to the death," the young Mohawk soldier agreed, bumping back.

"Or not," Louis said, unable to keep a straight face any longer.

"Not, for sure." The other man chuckled, his round face splitting into a wide, friendly smile.

The two of them turned to look at Louis's fellow members of Company E and began to laugh.

"Boys," Louis said, "you just been introduced to Indian humor."

There was a moment's pause as his four friends took in what had just happened. Then Joker raised his palm up to his chin. "Boys," he said, "I do believe we have just been paid back for all our teasing." Then he too began to laugh and the others joined in.

Louis turned and held out a hand. "Louis Nolette from St. Francis."

"Artis Cook," the young Mohawk said, "from St. Regis."

The handshake he returned was unlike that of a white man. His grasp was as relaxed as Louis's, neither turning their loose clasp into a contest of strength or a means of proving their manliness by crushing the other's fingers. It had been a long time since Louis had felt a handshake like the one Artis returned to him.

"Good to meet you," Artis added.

"You too," Louis said. Then he turned to his friends. "Thank you," he said.

"Boys," Artis said, "I thank you too, even if all you could find for me was an Abenaki. But seeing as how my grampa was an Abenaki himself—we Mohawks have been known to make mistakes—I guess he's just as good as any of my relatives."

"Or as bad," Louis said, "eh?"

"Eh!" Artis guffawed.

Louis grinned, knowing that he was making his white friends as confused as he was happy. He was letting a part of himself be seen that he had kept bottled up inside for so long.

Artis snapped his fingers. "Hey, would you boys like to go swimmin'? I have found a perfect swimmin' hole not far from here. Just down the hill from where my company is camped."

"Not me," a voice said loudly.

To Louis's surprise it was Merry. He was backing away, holding up both hands.

"Merry, lad," Devlin said, grabbing at the small soldier's sleeve. "Why say nay? Wouldn't y' like to wash away the stink of sweat and battle and blood that's on you as sure as it is on us all. You could take your clothes off and wash them good for a change."

"No! I can't. I . . . I'm afraid of water." Merry's eyes were strange as he tried to pull free. He looked at Louis pleadingly.

"Songbird," Louis said.

Devlin let go of Merry's sleeve. As soon as he did, Merry turned and ran away from them.

Louis shook his head. *What's wrong with him? He's been just about my best friend and now he runs away like that. Is he that shy to be seen with his clothes off? Or is it something else. Is he jealous about my finding another Indian to talk to?*

Artis looked just as confused as the rest of them. He lifted up his hands. "Well," he said.

"Swimming," Louis replied. "We're going swimming."

CHAPTER FIFTEEN
HEALING LEAVES

Sunday, May 15, 1864

The swimming spot Artis Cook led them to was a shallow, willow-shaded pond fed by a little stream.

"Start of the war," he said as they floated in the placid pool, "lots of us tried to join up. Even those of us like me who was too young. Even now, I'm only seventeen. Though you know how it is with white men. All us Indians look alike to 'em. Most can't tell if we're fourteen or forty."

Louis turned his head to the side. Kirk, Devlin, and Belaney were piling a rock dam at the head of the pool to try to make it more than neck deep. Not that they were making much headway. They were spending more time splashing water at each other than working.

"I know," Louis said.

"But you know what they told us then? Said it was a white man's war. Us Indians was not needed. It'd be over in a week or two. We just nodded, went back home, and waited. Once that week turned into two years, they come to beg us to join up! Isn't this a white man's war, we asked? Ain't our skins still brown? But we only teased 'em for a while before we took pity on 'em and said we was ready to serve."

Artis and two cousins had signed up together six months ago. Both cousins had been injured in the Wilderness. They were still at the Brigade Hospital.

"Not to have any limbs sawed off," Artis explained. "Cousin Andrew Cook had most of the hair on his head burnt off, even his eyebrows. Cousin Albert Cook, he is sure to have a hitch in his get-along once he starts walking again. I have visited 'em twice. They figure to be back on the line before mid-summer."

He turned, took a few lazy strokes, then rolled onto his back.

"Got any relatives in the battle, Nolette?"

"None," Louis said. "My mother, she is all the close family I have. My father, he was a soldier when he was young. He fought for the Americans against the British in 1812."

Is that another reason I joined the army? Because my father did so himself?

He kicked his feet in the water, making little waves.

"But he came back after the war. Then it was as a lumberjack that he worked. That's the reason I know how to swim. Papa said he saw many a man on the river who could ride the logs but never learned to swim a stroke and would drown if he fell in and there was no one there to pull him out. Although swimming did not help him, no, for he died on a log drive. I have some cousins, but they are all back at St. Francis. My mother, she is both a basket-maker and knows medicine. I joined up while we were in the States selling our baskets. At Troy it was, you know the town? At the time it seemed to me like the right thing to do. I don't know. What do you think, eh?"

Louis paused to take a breath. It was the longest speech he'd made since joining the army. Having another Indian to converse with seemed to make words flow out of him like the sap from a maple tree in the spring.

"You're a talkative one," Artis observed. "Ain't you?"

"No!" Louis said. Then he began to laugh, so hard that he breathed in a mouthful of water.

They slogged back to shore and sat on the bank in their long johns to let the sun dry them out before they put their clothes back on. Bull, Joker, and Songbird climbed up to join them. As his friends sat down, Louis shifted himself to the side and winced. He'd put his palm down on a sharp stone.

"Let me see that, Nolette," Artis said.

Louis held out his hand, palm up.

Artis nodded, then pulled on his pants and his boots. "Wait here."

He ran up the slope and soon came back holding a broad-leafed plant he'd uprooted.

"My auntie uses this," he explained. "She knows medicine like your mother. This is one the white men brought, which is why it takes over wherever it grows. Good for burns. Don't worry. I remembered to say *Niaweh*, thank you, when I pulled it up."

Louis took the plant from Artis Cook's hands. It was new to him, but he had seen it before. Just as it had appeared in his vision of his mother, fuzzy blue flowers bobbed above the green leaves.

Oleohneh nigawes. Thank you, my mother, he thought as he squeezed green juice from the leaves into the seared skin of his left hand.

"That helping some?" Artis asked.

"Yup," Louis replied.

Joker chuckled. "Don't expect more than a word or two from our friend Louis," he jibed. "He is our company's stoic redman. Getting him to give a speech is like trying to squeeze blood from a stone."

Louis raised one eyebrow as he looked over at Artis.

Artis nodded back.

"What are you Indians grinning about?" Joker said.

"Nothing," Louis replied.

"Everything," Artis added.

Then, while Louis's friends from Company E tried to figure out what was so funny, the two of them laughed till tears came to their eyes.

CHAPTER SIXTEEN

THE IRISHMAN AND THE INDIAN

Sunday, May 15, 1864

The time to themselves Flynn had told them to take was short-lived. No sooner had they returned from their swim than the order came to re-form their companies.

Artis Cook was with another New York regiment. Chances were they'd be close enough to see each other after the battle. Providing they survived it.

"Good luck on you, Nolette," Artis said, shaking Louis's hand. "Lord watch over you—as our old priest up at St. Regis says."

"You, too, Cook. *Olipamkaani*. Travel well."

And now, long after midnight, they were marching along yet another muddy and rutted road.

Sergeant Flynn, who'd chosen to walk beside Louis, was in an expansive mood.

"I've been thinkin' on something, Louis, m'lad."

Thinkin', Louis said to himself, *means I'm about to hear one of Flynn's lectures. His legs and his lungs both of iron must be made.*

The sergeant leaned closer. "Now, me son, this is for yer ears alone. I'm hoping that it's not crazy ye'll be thinkin' me, but I have been cogitatin' upon this for some time. And what I have concluded is that ye Indians and we Irish are one and the same."

One and the same? What white man has ever said that to me before?

The image of the gang of boys throwing stones at them as he and his mother came into town returned to Louis's mind.

Sergeant Flynn cleared his throat.

"Now, I'm not talking about that common kinship of humanity that we all share, ye and me and all those poor deluded Rebels and even those whose skins are as dark as the pitch-black of midnight. That common humanity is nothing to scorn, begorrah. For like Shakespeare's Shylock said, if ye prick us we all do bleed, and I've never seen a man of any race whose blood is anything but red. We all breathe in the same air. We eat the same and sleep the same and our bodies have those same private functions, each and every man."

Flynn tapped himself on the chest and then reached over to thud his broad hand against Louis's shoulder.

"It's the same mix of meat and blood and bone in us all, every one. But it's more than that upon my mind. What I've been thinking on is that there's a deeper bond between us, lad. There's a common thread sewn between those of us who come from the dear lost soil of the Emerald Isle and those like ye whose homeland is the earth beneath our feet. D'ye know what it is?"

Flynn paused.

No need for me to make a reply, Louis said to himself. It was clear that the Irishman would do enough talking for both. Plus Flynn seemed to understand better than most how Louis could answer a question by listening.

"Arghhh," the sergeant from Killarny said, his voice half growl and half sigh. "It's the cloth of history into which we've both been sewn, the red-haired Irishman and the red-skinned Indian. Put those histories side by side and it'll be the thing itself and its image in the mirror. Y'know how the English came over here and tried t' wipe out yer people? Well, they tried t' do it t' us first. Cromwell and his evil band of murderers hoped t' wipe our race off the face of the land like we was no more than dirt on the floor. Because the color of our hair was different—they said we was savages and vermin and a curse upon the land, better dead and gone. We fought back against them as men fight, hand t' hand, as brave and foolish as ever a warrior might be. But they cut us down with their finer weapons and their greater numbers. They even bought off some of our own people with gold and promises and turned 'em t' take up arms against us. And does that sound familiar t' you, boyo?

"Then they gave our land t' their own people and pushed us into the roughest, hardest places to live, sometimes allowin' us t' work for them, for a few potatoes and a crust of bread t' survive upon. And then when they could not kill us all or force us all t' leave the land, they tried t' force us all t' speak their tongue and not the beautiful Gaelic that my sainted parents made sure I cut me eyeteeth upon. *Erin go bragh.*

"Then they saw another use for us and that was in their armies, trusting we'd show the same courage we did when we fought against 'em. And we did it in spite of all that history. We did it t' prove to them the kind of men we were and to make a place in the world for us and our children to come."

Flynn's voice caught.

Louis felt a similar lump in his own throat.

He understands. And so do I.

Bad as it had been and as bad as he knew it would be in the days ahead, Louis knew then that he was in the right place. It was not just a white man's battle that they were fighting. There was no place he'd rather be than in the presence of his sergeant whose words touched the heart of his heart.

What would Jean Nolette have thought of Sergeant Michael Flynn?

He would have shaken his hand.

They plodded along in silence for a mile or more before Fynn cleared his throat and spat.

"And here we great fools both are," the sergeant said as they began to labor up a slope. "In this brigade, that's always called upon when there's work t' be done that is desperate, absurd, or forlorn. And what do we get in the end? A small bit of ground t' bury our bones? A handful of coin and perhaps a bit of ribbon and metal to wear on our chest? Or the right to call ourselves men?"

Flynn raised his arm.

"Column halt!" he called out.

They stopped, more or less. Some of the exhausted men who'd been walking in a half sleep kept on for a step or two before being stopped by the backs of the soldiers in front of them.

They'd reached a high hilltop. A line of lights flickered below them from the farther hills beyond a wide field. Hundreds of Southern lanterns, candles, and campfires burning behind their entrenchments.

And there's the line we'll be attacking at dawn without the benefit of a wink of sleep or a bite of food. Two hundred yards of open ground to cross while being pounded by artillery and struck by a storm of bullets.

Louis looked to their left. The rest of Hancock's Union forces were coming up, Artis Cook's company among them. The Irish Brigade and the Corcoran Legion would hold the extreme right.

Louis sighed.

"So, lad," Flynn asked, "what do we do, the Mick and the Indian?"

Louis answered that question with spoken words.

"The best we can, sir."

CHAPTER SEVENTEEN
MARY O'SHEA

Wednesday, May 18, 1864

The shell that whistled by was ten feet above him. Not that close, but Louis kept his head down anyway.

Doesn't sound like a Napoleon, he thought. *Too small.*

Napoleons was what everyone on both sides called the Model 1857 twelve-pounder field guns. Favorite artillery pieces for both North and South, they were smooth-bored weapons that could throw a twelve-pound shell, solid shot, or canister 1,600 yards.

Louis crawled nearer, keeping low. The half-light before dawn and the way the land folded like the crease in a palm made it simple to stay out of sight. He reached the ridge across from the Confederate gun crews that had begun firing on E Company at 5:00 a.m.

Louis raised up, a finger's width at a time, squinted through the binoculars Flynn had lent him for his scouting mission. He focused in on trees, the back of a horse, then an artillery wagon.

Just as I figured. Six-pounders.

It wasn't that hard to find them from his vantage point. As always, the artillery had been placed on a ridge behind and above the Rebel line. The four Southern guns and their crews were silhouetted by the near-dawn sky, a lighter blue than the dark sky to the west.

Guns had to be in plain sight for their crews to see where their shots fell and adjust their next rounds. But they were an easy target for counter-battery fire. Gun crews were often the earliest casualties. And even if the shells fired at them missed, they could still hit the nearby munitions wagons. A man with a gun crew had to just stand upright, a target for small arms fire. He had no weapon other than that big hungry gun that he kept feeding with shells and cannonballs.

Louis watched, fascinated.

The eight-man crew that moved around each gun seemed to be doing a dance. Deadly, but graceful, getting off four rounds in a minute. One crew member cleaned the bore with a long-handled rammer. Another handed the cartridge to the third man who inserted it into the muzzle where the first man could shove it in with the rammer. Behind the gun a fourth gunner cut and inserted the fuse as a fifth and sixth brought up more heavy cartridges. The chief of the gun crew checked the aim, raised his hand. The eighth man pulled the lanyard. A dense cloud of white smoke suddenly appeared at the muzzle as the cannon violently recoiled six feet to the rear. Half a second later, Louis heard the thunder-clap boom, close enough to make his ears ring.

Must be ten times louder where that gun crew stands.

Most men in the artillery were not only easy targets, they were also deafened by their work.

I would, no way, want to be in the artillery. That work it is not just too dangerous. It is too dang noisy.

He lowered himself down and began to crawl backward.

"Well?" Sergeant Fynn asked.

"Model 1841 six-pounders," Louis said. "Four of them."

"I'd thought they was not Napoleons by the sound of them," Flynn replied. "A bit too tinny."

In battle, the sergeant's ears were as accurate as most men's eyes. Better, in fact, when the smoke and dust blinded your vision.

"If ye don't know which way t' go, then march toward the thunder," Flynn would say. "Ye can do that with yer eyes closed."

The sergeant turned to the men lined up in the shadows of the pine woods behind him. A shower of needles and small branches fell on their shoulders as a shell went whistling through the treetops.

"'Tis lucky we are today," Flynn said. "All they have up there is four little peashooters. And as ye can clearly see, our dear Rebel friends are shooting high as they always do." The sergeant chuckled. "There's not an artillery man in the South kin hit the side of a hill. Now with the dawn coming behind 'em and the blessed dark of the west behind us, we'll be seeing 'em better. Their sharpshooters'll be cursing their bad luck at not being able to find a target. Now, with the Corcoran Legion by our side, who kin stop the boys of the Irish Brigade?"

"No one at all, sir," Devlin's voice called out from the crowd of men whose faces were hidden by the darkness.

"No Johnny Reb," Kirk said.

"Not even the divvil hisself," Belaney affirmed.

Their voices sound as eager as if we are being asked to take a walk through a park in spring.

Despite all they'd been through in the past days, no matter that they had seen so many friends fall, the spirit of the 69th that day was high.

It makes no sense.

Yet Louis felt his own spirits raise and his heart pound in pride.

"On the double quickstep then. When they see our green flag and realize who's coming at them, they'll run."

Two hundred yards to cross. Shots whistled overhead.

A hundred yards. Shells began to fall among them.

Fifty yards. Despite the poor light, sharpshooters behind their breastworks were now picking out targets. Grapeshot and rifle balls were reaping a deadly harvest.

As he trotted forward, Louis saw men fall to either side of him. But their own rifles and the Union cannon were taking a toll on the Rebel ranks. Minié balls whistled over his head. Shells burst to either side, but he was untouched. As he neared the first entrenched position, the shots were fewer, the cannons silent. Louis leaped up, grabbed at a branch that was thrust out of the parapet, and pulled himself over.

The rifle pit on the other side was almost empty. Only three wounded men in gray with their rifles on the ground and their hands in the air. The main body of the Rebels had abandoned the position and were retreating through the pines.

"After them!" a man with a captain's bars on his uniform shouted as he ran. Louis recognized him as one of the officers of the 69th. Captain Blake.

Louis and all those of the Legion and the Brigade who could still run or hobble or limp followed Blake. Their line was ragged, but they crossed the uneven ground and picked their way through the pines.

Another line of fortifications, larger than the first they'd just taken, rose up ahead. The Rebels had fallen back behind it. A withering fire burst forth at them. Bark flew from tree trunks, blood misted the air.

"*Re-form!*" Captain Blake shouted.

"Re-form ranks," Sergeant Flynn repeated, his words echoed down the blue mass of men.

Louis quickly looked around. All the faces were strange to him. The soldiers from several regiments were rallying together behind the captain and sergeant at their head, unmindful of the tempest of bullets, the shells falling like driving rain.

A flag bearer next to Louis grabbed at his hip and fell. Louis's left hand closed around the pole before their green flag with its Irish harp struck the soil. It was the only color on their part of the line. You needed a flag to rally the regiment.

I'm a target now for every Rebel sharpshooter.

Louis started to lift the flag higher.

Captain Blake was too quick for him. "I'll take that, soldier," Blake said with a smile.

Grasping the pole of the flag with both hands, Blake climbed to the highest point on the work and waved it back and forth.

"Come on, boys, and I will show you how to fight!" he called out in a clear voice that carried like a song.

Another sergeant, not Flynn, but a noncom from B Company, stepped forward to take the flag from the captain's hands as Blake made his way to the front, leading them toward the mass of gray-clad soldiers gathering before the entrenchments for a counterattack.

It seems as if the bullet's not been made that can strike him. His bravery's a suit of armor.

But as Louis thought those words, Captain Blake dropped down to one knee. Or rather he fell to the place where a knee had once been. A minié ball had struck, leaving a great wound that showed splintered bone for a heartbeat before it was covered by the gush of blood. A lieutenant leaped to Blake's side, tried to stop the bleeding with a tourniquet. A carrying party formed, but as they lifted the wounded captain onto a stretcher, one and then another of the bearers were struck down by the fire from the oncoming counterattack.

Blake propped himself up on the stretcher to wave one arm. "Save yourselves," he shouted, teeth gritted against the pain, face pale from loss of blood. "The enemy's upon us!"

As so often happens in battle, the rush of men, the sound of guns, and the clouds of smoke washed over Louis then. Time passed. Whether minutes or hours, no one could say. They drove back not just one counterattack, but too many to count. A field of fallen men lay between them and the Confederate ranks gathered behind the next line of trees, showing no sign of another assault.

Somehow, the sun had leaped across the sky. It was well past midday. A hand rose up in the no-man's-land between the two armies.

"Water," a voice called out from among the dead and wounded.

"I know that voice," someone who was standing next to Louis said.

He turned to look. It was Merry. He and Devlin, Kirk, and Belaney had all found their way to this same spot in the line where their sergeant stood, solid as an oak. Somehow, Flynn had gathered them the way a mother hen does her chicks.

"Water," the man called again in a voice weakened by wounds. "Will no one bring me a drink of water before I die?" The man lifted himself up on one elbow. His uniform showed him to be a Union captain.

"Tom O'Shea," Merry called, his voice more high and shrill than Louis had heard before. "Tom! Is it you?"

Merry grabbed the canteen that hung by Louis's side and pulled it free. Then, before anyone else could move or speak, Merry was over the embankment, down into the rifle pit, and then up and out of it as quickly as a young deer bounding through the forest. Rebel shots were being fired as Merry ran, but the little private paid them no mind and none struck home.

Louis tried to follow. Devlin and Kirk held him back.

"It's a fine heroic thing the lad is doing," Devlin said, not letting go of Louis's arm, "and it's worthy of a song. But there's no place for you in this ballad, Chief."

"Tom," Merry called. "Tom."

"Whose voice is that?" the injured man answered.

Somehow, though their words were not loud, a trick of the way the land lay or the clarity of the air made the two voices carry to all ears. There was pride on the one side for the bravery the young soldier was showing and respect on the other side for that same courage. Rebel marksmen were grounding their weapons and standing up to watch.

"Who are you?" the wounded captain said as Merry reached him. "Am I dreaming?"

Merry dropped down on one knee, placing one hand behind

the wounded captain's shoulders and holding the canteen to his lips with the other.

"It's me, Tom, drink this."

The man drank and then jerked back. "You?" he said, his voice startled. "How can it be? In a uniform? And your hair? Where's your beautiful long hair?"

"Tom O'Shea." The little private was weeping now in a most unmanly way. "I did it to be close to you. Can you forgive me?"

"Mary," Captain O'Shea said, his hand caressing her face. "My Mary."

Louis was not sure how many realized what they were seeing, but he knew.

How is it all of us was fooled for so long?

He looked over at Sergeant Flynn.

"Hold your fire!" the sergeant suddenly bellowed in a voice that echoed off the hills. "That wee lad is a lass. Put up your guns."

Flynn was at the top of the parapet now, waving one arm in the air and pointing the other toward the stunned men in gray.

"D' ye not see 'tis the man's own wife?"

On the field before them Mary O'Shea had taken off her private's coat and unwound the roll of cloth she'd bound around her chest to hide the curve of her bosom. She began tearing the cloth into bandages.

By the time she'd bound her husband's wound, a party of stretcher bearers had reached her, Louis and Flynn among them. Not a shot came from either side as men stood and watched, guns by their sides. And who among them was not thinking of the dear ones they'd left behind? For one blessed moment, all thoughts of fighting left that field.

In the surgeon's tent, no one seemed to be able to say a word until Surgeon O'Meagher had finished his examination of the weak but still conscious man.

"No need for amputation of any limbs," O'Meagher said to Captain O'Shea. "Clean flesh wounds in both arms and legs. You would have, of course, exsanguinated had you been left to lie for another hour. With proper care you'll live a long life—though your career as a soldier is over."

"I'll care for him," Mary said.

How could I have ever thought her anything but a woman? Louis thought. Now that he knew she was a woman, she no longer looked so young. *Much older than me, probably as old as twenty-four.*

"Private Merry," a deep Irish voice said. It was, of course, Flynn. "I'm afraid ye'll no longer be able to be part of this man's army. Ye'll have to turn in yer weapon and kit and uniform, and forfeit what pay ye have comin', I'm sorry to say. Ye were a fine soldier."

"Yes, sir," Mary O'Shea said, coming to attention and snapping a salute as she did so and then breaking into a grin. "I'll gladly give up this wool uniform, sir. But I shall miss my musket."

Flynn turned to Captain O'Shea, who hardly seemed to have heard the sergeant's speech. His eyes were on his wife, a look on his face that combined love and awe.

"Sir," Flynn said, "I know it's out of place for me to speak this way to a superior officer and all, but I need to say it. Ye take care of yer wife and cherish her and ne'er say a hard word for what she's done or ye'll be hearing from Liam Flynn."

"Sergeant," Captain O'Shea said, "it's less I'd be thinking of you had you not said that." He weakly lifted one hand to shake Flynn's. "You have my word as surely as my dear wife has my everlasting love."

Mary O'Shea grasped Louis by the elbow and pulled him over. "Tom, this is Louis. He's a fine lad. He has been my best friend these weeks and as good a friend as any soldier could have wanted."

Captain O'Shea turned his eyes toward Louis. "So you watched over my Mary in battle, boy?"

Louis nodded.

More like she watched over me, he thought, but words weren't coming to his lips.

Tom O'Shea let go of Flynn's hand and reached toward Louis to grasp the same arm that Mary held. For the first time there was a hint of a smile on the wounded captain's face. "So, my wife's best friend, would you do me the honor of repeating your name?"

"Louis, Private Louis Nolette, sir."

"Louis? That's a good name, isn't it, Mary? A good name to give a son if the Lord should so bless us in the years to come?"

"Yes, my dear Tom," Mary said. Her face was bright with happiness, one hand on her husband's shoulder and the other on Louis's arm. "Yes."

CHAPTER EIGHTEEN
IN THE RIVER

Friday, May 20, 1864

"So," Flynn said, "there's a use for cavalry after all."

The sergeant carefully folded the newspaper and put it down gently on the log bench.

As if it's a butterfly whose wings might be damaged by rough handling.

Louis hadn't really taken notice of it before. But, come to think of it, Flynn was always like that with anything with words on it. It didn't matter if it was a Bible, a magazine, a newspaper, or even a leaflet. The printed word seemed to be a sacred thing to their sergeant

"And what would that be?" Corporal Hayes asked, limping over to grab the newspaper from the bench.

"Gently, Corporal," Flynn said. "You'll tear the dear thing. Just look there near the middle of the first page."

Hayes sat down as if his legs were made of wood.

Still stiff from being clubbed by rifle butts.

The corporal rubbed his equally bruised chin gingerly with one hand before opening the paper.

Those Rebs who captured Hayes were none too gentle. But our corporal himself returned the favor.

Because the corporal's captors had neglected to have him give his word that he would not try an escape, he had waited till his captors were distracted by a shell bursting near them. The thought of being shot while trying to get away appealed to him more than being sent to Andersonville. Grabbing a gun from one man, the corporal had kicked another in the belly and slugged a third in the chin with the musket barrel. Then Hayes hightailed it through the trees.

It had been near dark, but even then he might not have made it had he not been near a small rapid-flowing stream. Without hesitating, Hayes had jumped in and been carried around the bend. It had taken him two days to find his way back to what was left of E Company.

Louis smiled at the memory of the return of their formerly lost noncom. Corporal Hayes had thought to surprise them, but had ended more surprised himself. That their numbers were so diminished was sad but not shocking. That one of their men had been a woman shook him more than his own capture and bangs and bruises.

"The wee lad was a lass?" Hayes said in a voice that brought a grin to Sergeant Flynn's face. "The wee lad was a lass?"

In the day and a half the corporal had been back with them he'd repeated his bemused question innumerable times. One minute he'd be pounding a piece of hardtack with a stone to break it into pieces that his sore jaw could handle and the next he would pause and look up.

"The wee lad was a lass?"

Even last night, settled into his tent, other men snoring about him, his voice had broken the still of the night every two or three hours with those same six words.

"The wee lad was a lass?"

Louis wondered if the sergeant's calling Hayes's attention to the newspaper was not just a way to turn the corporal's mind toward something else.

Hayes's brow furrowed as he studied the paper, leaning his head close to the page. Unlike Flynn, the corporal was a deliberate reader whose lips moved as he sounded out each word. He finished a sentence and looked up.

"General Jeb Stuart is dead?" Hayes asked.

"Aye," Flynn replied. "Shot and killed dead by one of Sheridan's men in a clash between their cavalry units. I heard word of it two days ago, but seein' it in this copy of the *Richmond Enquirer* so generously given to me by one of our prisoners—ye can trust that it's gospel truth. They are mournin' his loss in Richmond. 'Tis the heaviest blow they've took since Stonewall Jackson."

Flynn slapped his thighs with his broad palm and stood up.

"So, as I said, there seems to be a bit of use for cavalry after all. And that is t' lessen the number of cavalrymen on the other side. For an enemy cavalryman is worse—though only by a hairsbreadth—than one of our own."

Flynn carefully extricated the newspaper from Hayes's grasp, folded it again, and stowed it in his pack. Then the sergeant stared off into the distance, one broad hand on his chest, his fingers tapping against the buttons of his coat. The Virginia sun was beating down from a cloudless sky and Flynn reached up to wipe the sweat from his brow. It was so quiet in this lull between the fighting that had lasted for over a day now, you could hear the trickling voice of the North Ana River as it rippled over the stones down into a little pool a hundred yards from them.

As the sun reflected off its surface, that pool caught Louis's eye. *Almost the same as the one Artis led me and Kirk and Belaney and Devlin to before the battle.*

All five of them frolicking like little boys in the water. He smiled at the thought that all five of them were still among those who could breathe and walk on their own feet. Not among the lost. True, he'd lost Merry—Mary O'Shea. He was going to miss Merry dreadfully. But the thought of the happiness she'd found made him feel warm inside. He thought of his mother's words: "We never know what each day will bring us. Be thankful for every small blessing from Bon Dieu."

The boy he'd been only weeks ago hadn't understood those words at all. Now, though, they were easier to understand.

He'd seen Artis just last evening. Both of them on picket duty—Artis to the left of his company's line and Louis to E Company's right. They'd been able to exchange a few quick words.

But none about the fight they'd survived.

"You bark-eating Abernakis ever play marbles?" Artis asked.

"A sight better than most Mohawks," Louis answered. "But I don't have a marble with me."

Artis jiggled the leather sack that hung at his side. "Plenty here to loan you some till I win 'em back. You know us Mohawks always win when we come up against you Abernakis."

"In a pig's eye," Louis replied, keeping his face straight for another moment before breaking into a grin as wide as the one Artis wore. They'd made plans to get together after mess the next day if things stayed quiet.

It would be good to do something so far removed from the grim business of war. He was looking forward also to surprising Artis with the news that one of the soldiers he'd introduced his new friend to had actually been a woman in disguise. Although Artis might already have heard. The tale of Mary O'Shea, the warrior lass, was making its way from one regiment to the next.

"Hmm," Sergeant Flynn said loudly to himself, his fingers drumming again on his buttons.

It drew Louis out of his reverie. The other men of E Company pricked up their ears as well. Something was on their sergeant's mind when he made a sound like that. Clasping his chin in one hand and grasping his elbow with the other, the big Irishman lapsed back into momentary silence.

The men of E Company held their breath. Flynn getting quiet like that meant for sure that something was being planned.

Whomp! The sergeant's broad palms slapped together like a thunder clap.

"Aye!" Flynn exclaimed, raising up the index fingers of both meaty hands. "That's the ticket! Ye need to rid yerselves of the stink and stench of battle. And who among ye but our good Corporal Hayes has had himself a proper bath? Form up, lads. It's down to the river with ye all."

When they reached the riverbank, Flynn looked them over. "Now, who among ye can swim?"

Half of the men raised their hands.

"Fine," Flynn said. "Then ye who know the ways of the otter and the finny fish may keep an eye on the others t' be sure they don't drown. Because each and every one of ye is going into that water. Wait! Every stitch of yer clothing is coming off before ye go in."

Halfway through pulling off his underwear, the first time he'd fully undressed since putting on his uniform, Louis had a thought.

I've never seen any of the other men of E Company naked before—nor has our sergeant.

Louis shook his head in amusement. His own skin was an even earthen brown. But the other naked privates were a patchwork of colors—sunburned red on their necks, tanned on their faces and hands, and pale as plucked chickens where clothing had kept away the sun. Some were covering their parts with hands or caps.

"Attention!" Sergeant Flynn barked.

The men snapped straight, hands at their sides. Sergeant Flynn walked past them eyeing each closely. "Fine," he said at last. "At ease, *men*, and into the river with ye."

The water of the pool was cool and clean and a blessed relief, indeed. As Louis floated on his back, looking up at the blue sky, the other men laughed and splashed at one another as if they knew nothing of being soldiers hardened by combat. Up on the bank their clothes lay in piles.

Take off our uniforms and what do we become? Boys again.

Louis chuckled. *But not girls. Not a wee lass among us.*

Sergeant Flynn's bathing party had made sure of that.

CHAPTER NINETEEN
SKILLYGALLEE AND SONG

Monday, May 30, 1864

Almost as soon as the men had dried themselves and put their uniforms back on the order came down that they were to break camp. Grant had ordered Meade to lead the Army of the Potomac across the Mattapony River, so Louis's plan for marbles with Artis was not to be for now. A bigger game was about to be played in which men, and not balls of clay, were the pieces to be shot at.

They forded the Mattapony after another night march. Then it was across the North Ana River, where they engaged Lee's grayback boys. All in a heat so great that Louis felt as if the buttons on his sack coat were about to melt.

Then it was fall back to find the enemy's right flank and get around it.

Though it seems as if we're wandering like the Hebrew tribes in the wilderness.

Cross the North Ana a second time. Turn toward Hanover-town and over the Pamunkey River to find the enemy at Tolopotomy Creek.

Shoot and shovel. Don't try to make sense of it. Just do what you're told.

"Move out, men!"

This time to Hanover Court House, where more soldiers in gray waited, dug in north of the Chickahominy River.

So many rivers that my head is swimming. But they say we're now only ten miles from Richmond, the Southern capital. Take Richmond and we'll have won the war.

And then, finally, after more than a week of marching and digging trenches, skirmishing, falling back, moving forward to dig in yet again, they came to a halt.

Corporal Hayes stroked his mustache as he looked over the top of their trench toward the heavily fortified Confederate lines a mile away. He turned to nod down at Louis and his mess mates laboring below him. "Dig in lads, build up them walls."

"Lads?" Joker said in a low voice as he nudged Louis with his elbow. "Moles is more like it."

Louis nodded as he levered up yet another spadeful of red earth. Moles.

"Corporal, sir, do you know the name of this place?" Joker asked, leaning for a moment on his shovel.

"Cold Harbor, I'm told," Hayes replied in a monotone. "Remember that name, so you can say you were at the place where the battle was fought that broke the back of the rebellion?"

Strange. He's not saying those words as if he believes them. More like a question. In fact, it seems as if everything Hayes says since he escaped from the Rebs has been a question. As if he's doubting everything around him now.

Hayes gestured vaguely in the direction of the Rebel entrenchment that stretched for miles in each direction.

"The South's worn out, so Grant says. All Lee has the heart to do is dig in."

Dug in like an old wounded wolf. What was it mon père *said? No animal more dangerous than a hurt one in his lair.* The thought brought a tight feeling to his gut. *Lee and his boys are just waiting for us fools to try to go in after them.*

"Wore out?" Belaney growled.

"So the general says," Corporal Hayes replied. Then he wandered off down the trench, still stroking his mustache.

Not even trying to keep his head down, even though there might be a sharpshooter over there who could hit a man from that range. Is it that our corporal is no longer afraid of dying? Or is it that this all no longer seems real to him?

"Cold Harbor," Belaney said, twisting his face as if the words hurt his mouth.

"Hot Harbor, more like," Kirk said, tapping his spade against the floor of the trench. "Fill this hole with water, the sun'd heat it up enough to boil potatoes."

"Potatoes," Devlin said, looking up from the skillet where he was taking his turn fixing their dinner. Since Merry's departure, Songbird had drawn the short straw to be the man lugging the iron pan.

"Potatoes," he repeated, his voice wistful. "Now there's a word that none of our commissary men seem to have in their vocabulary these days. It's naught but sowbelly, worm castles, and water for us poor boys in the Irish Brigade."

"Water?" Joker said. "So that's what you call the liquid we've been drinking that's dark enough to paint a barn?"

"Ah, but it makes for a fine cup of coffee," Devlin said. "Soldier's coffee, indeed."

"And what is soldier's coffee, might I inquire?" Belaney asked.

"Coffee," Devlin said, "strong enough that when you stick a spoon in it, the spoon stands up."

"Not as strong as lumberman's coffee," Louis said, surprising himself and the others by joining in.

"And how strong would that be, Chief?" Kirk asked, playing along.

"Lumberman's coffee," Louis said, keeping his face straight, "you stick a spoon in it and the spoon melts."

The others laughed as if the old joke was as fine and new as a shiny silver dollar. Everyone seemed quick to laugh now, even at the smallest and weakest of jokes. A hard, nervous sort of laughter that died as quickly as it was born.

Like the other morning as they had been trudging along yet another dusty red track. Someone in the line of march had seen a three-legged dog by the side of the road and shouted out, "Wull, there's Jeff Davis."

Within moments that comment about the sorry three-legged stray being the president of the Confederacy had gone all the way back down the line. About every man in the regiment was guffawing at it whether he'd seen that dog or not. Some had laughed so hard they almost choked. A few had even fallen down on the ground and had to be helped back to their feet.

Devlin poked at the fire under the dented iron skillet.

"How's our dinner doing?" Belaney asked, coming over to look. "You've got the last of me salt pork in the pot."

"Now, Bull," Devlin said, "don't be complaining. You know that if you'd kept it in your pack, that sowbelly would just be oozing grease and rotting in the weather instead of part of a fine skillygallee."

Skillygallee. Nothing more than hardtack and water and salt pork boiled into mushy slop.

Louis thought, and not for the first time, about the meals his mother made for them as they traveled from place to place. *Rabbit, that makes a good stew. Muskrat too. Deer, beaver. Shucks, me, I would be glad for as much as a squirrel.*

But with all these men in blue and gray scouring the land, every animal that could be eaten had already been consumed or fled for its life. He'd heard the Johnnies were even eating the rattlesnakes. Any critter big as a field mouse was taking its life in its paws if it ventured near the Rebel lines.

Songbird tapped the bayonet he was using as a stirring spoon against the side of the skillet. "Done as it'll ever be," he sighed. "But don't expect much of it. There's no man can mix up a batch of skillygallee like our dear Housewife could."

"There's a fact," Kirk agreed. He dropped his shovel, took a spoon from his coat pocket, and scooped some of the gray mixture onto the tin plate he'd pulled from his pack. "And now our fine lad who made an even finer lass'll be cooking for her husband. Chicken and gravy with dumplings, most likely."

As the others helped themselves to the sorry stew, Louis filled their tin cups with coffee from the pot placed on a flat stone next to the fire.

"Boys," Kirk said, rising to his feet and lifting his coffee cup high where the light from the fire glittered off it, "here's to the finest man who never was."

Before the others could stand to voice their agreement, there came a sudden sound like the whining of a gnat.

Whang!

Coffee sprayed around the small circle of men as the cup went flying from Kirk's hand.

"Jesus, Mary, and Joseph!" Joker said, dropping down onto his back and grabbing his numbed fingers with his other hand. "Them Rebel snipers are going too far. It's one thing to knock a man's head off, but spilling his coffee is a low, uncivilized act."

"Did you notice," Devlin said, crawling over to pick up the dented cup and refill it for his comrade, "the pitch of that particular ball before it struck? Being a musician meself, I believe it swelled from E flat to an F and then dropped near to a D as it lost its velocity."

A distant rumble came from the heavens. For a moment, Louis thought it was guns before he recognized it as thunder. Just a month ago it would have been the opposite and he would not have confused the ancient voice of the Bedagiak with the brutal sound of cannons. All four of them were silent for a moment, looking up at the dark sky as they lay on their backs in the trench.

Finally, Songbird sighed. "And there was the bass drum of the Lord, sounding the counterpoint to the melody."

"So give us a song," Belaney said as he sat up.

And three weeks ago who would have imagined music was something that a man like that Bull Belaney would love.

The one-time claim jumper had shown himself to be a man of more depth and sentiment than anyone had expected. No fewer than four times in the last few weeks, Belaney had spent his spare cash not on sweets from the sutlers but sheet music, eager for the newest songs being penned. Not that he was alone. There were countless thousands of men eager to hear a song that might lift their hearts. Bull couldn't read the notes, but with Devlin's help he could puzzle out the words printed below them. And once Songbird had sung him the tune, Bull would always remember the melody.

"Bull's right," Kirk agreed. "After a fine batch of skillygallee we need a song to round off the festivities."

"What shall it be?" Songbird wiped off the skillet with a rag and tied it onto his pack. "'Rally Round the Flag, Boys'? 'After the Battle, Mother'?"

Belaney rummaged in his pack. "This one," he said.

Devlin scanned the name and illustration on the front of the folded sheet. "Good title." He opened it to study the tune, took a breath, and began to sing.

> "We are tenting tonight on the old camp ground.
> Give us a song to cheer
> our weary hearts with thoughts of home
> and friends we love so dear.
> Many are hearts that are weary tonight
> wishing for the war to cease.
> Many are the hearts that are looking to the right
> to see the dawn of Peace.
> Tenting tonight, tenting tonight,
> tenting on the old camp ground."

The second time around, Bull, then Kirk, then Louis, then even more of the other men who had been working in the darkness to each side of them joined in. Louis was never sure just how many voices finally raised together. A hundred? A thousand? But when they stopped, he heard what seemed to be an echo. Then he recognized it for what it was. Other voices from farther off had taken up the tune—Rebel soldiers whose minds and hearts and bodies were just as weary of war.

And as they sang, voices uniting the darkness, rain began to fall.

Not rain. Tears. Tears from our Great Creator's eyes. He knows what we are all soon to do.

CHAPTER TWENTY
AFTER COLD HARBOR

Saturday, June 4, 1864

Louis gritted his teeth as he tried to lever the log into place. An arrow of pain stabbed into the bruised small of his back. He wiped the moisture from his eyes with his other sleeve. His arm rustled against a sheet of paper stuck to his chest. He looked down at it in momentary confusion, read the words upside down.

Private Louis Nolette.

Who put that there?

He did. He'd printed those letters, pinned that paper in place a full day ago.

He pictured the scene again. Hundreds of other blue-coated soldiers carefully lettering their identities onto white sheets with a calmness that belied their fears. From the greenest private to the oldest veteran, they'd all known what would happen when the bugles blew the advance.

Cold Harbor. Not a port where ships might come in, although the sluggish Pamunkey River ran behind them. Cold Harbor had been the name of a white-framed tavern in a nearby grove. Now, though, it was the name of the nearby field of battle. Cold Harbor. A place that gave cold comfort, for sure.

Louis closed his eyes. He didn't want to see it, but the images came to him just the same.

Rain before dawn. After a night so hot that the downpour was a blessed relief to some. But Louis had another thought as heavy drops fell from thick clouds, obscuring all signs of sunrise.

Great Creator knows what is going to happen. He's closed the eyes of the sky so He doesn't have to watch.

"All-out assault?" Hayes said, gesturing at the steep hill ahead.

Too steep. Too much open ground to cross.

"Break through that line?" the corporal continued in the questioning monotone that had become his voice.

A short month ago Sergeant Flynn's right-hand man had been one of those neat, precise men who did as he was told and never felt the need to think deeply. Well-groomed as Flynn was rumpled, Hayes always had his hair combed, his red mustache exactly trimmed. But though he'd leap to Flynn's every command, he'd never seemed weak.

155

Now something's missing in Hayes. Still does as ordered. But there's a dark edge of doubt.

But who wouldn't have doubts, seeing those giant earthworks stretching all the way from the Chicahominy River to Totopotomoy Creek?

Every time we break through, their next fortification is just that much stronger.

"We far outnumber the forces left to Lee. Prisoners have told us that the ranks are so short of food, they're boiling their shoes to eat—if they're lucky enough to still have shoes. They'll crumble like a piece of day-old corn bread at our first attack. The whole war could be over by the weekend."

That was what Colonel Byrnes, their new commander, said.

Then the bugles sounded.

The Irish Brigade and all the rest, a full 50,000 men, surged forward.

"Huzzah!" men shouted. *"Huzzah!"*

Their shouts and thudding feet in quick step, flap of brigade and battalion flags in the winds, the occasional pop of a musket from their own ranks as some overeager soldier pulled a trigger out of sheer nervousness. But no enemy fire. Yet.

His breath burning because his throat was so tense, Louis trotted beside his friends.

Farther up the hill.

Farther still.

Were the Rebs truly there behind those earth walls? Or had

they retreated in fear of the great mass of determined men coming up the hill against them?

Less than fifty yards till we reach the works. We might . . .

Hundreds of black hats suddenly appeared above the dark earthworks. Like a shudder of lightning, the wall burst into flame. So many Southern rifles fired at once that it seemed more a volcanic blast than a volley. Then, less than a heartbeat later, the Southern artillery barrage began. Unlike other battles where Confederate gunners had a hard time finding the range, their aim was brutally accurate.

How long did it just take for 12,000 men in blue to be killed or wounded?

Things seemed to move around him in slow motion, but Louis knew it was all happening at a breathtaking pace. So many Rebel guns fired that men were struck not by one shot or two, but by half a dozen balls all at once.

Out of the corner of his eye, Louis saw the puffs of dust fogging out from uniforms as men were mowed down like wheat to either side. He tripped over a fallen body, lurched sideways, then was driven to his knees by two sledgehammer blows that struck low in the middle of his back.

His face pressing into the earth, dirt in his mouth, his arms flung out in front of himself.

Am I dead?

Somehow breath came back to his lungs. Hands tugged him up, lifted him to his feet, thrust the rifle back into his hands. Joker. Kirk. Bull.

Move, he told his feet. Thud of artillery. Ducking under the banshee screams of shells. Stumbling as the ground shakes like a badly laid board floor.

I'm alive. But how?

Hours later he'd discover that the tight-rolled rubber poncho on his back had stopped two minié balls.

Eight minutes. That was how long it took for most of the Union offensive to be stopped in its tracks. Those not hit by enemy fire went to their bellies, trying to scrape out rifle pits with hands, drinking cups, bayonets. Pinned down, desperate, unable to move forward or back. Bullets and shells thick as burning hail.

Not all stopped. The Brigade and the Legion pushed forward without pause. Though their ranks thinned, they pushed on, step by step up that endless hill.

A Gray soldier rose and raised a rifle. Louis hurled his body against the Reb, who fell back into the trench and was lost in the smoke.

"Brave work, boy," someone shouted at Louis.

Colonel James McMahon, 164th New York.

The colonel was holding the flag in both hands, planting it atop the entrenchment.

Should I salute, him being a superior officer?

A fool thought in the midst of battle, but before Louis could do anything—foolish or not—the smile on McMahon's face faded. His eyes rolled up, his legs folded beneath him.

Louis reached for the colonel as a spinning piece of hot metal from an exploding shell whistled by his ear. He found himself holding not the man, but the pole of that flag that had been planted. The colonel's torn body slumped at his feet. Someone took the flag from Louis's hand. Time to load and fire again and again.

How did we do it? Not only took that hill but held it two hours against one counterattack after another?

Only after the artillery was trained on them did they retreat. Eyes half-blind with sweat and smoke, blood and tears. Never running. Never turning their backs. Step by step, they fought their way back to rifle pits fifty yards from the enemy lines uphill.

There they stayed. Then "Bloody Grant," as some called him now, sent orders down for another assault. And a sort of miracle happened.

"Our own General Hancock, may the Saints preserve him," said Sergeant Flynn, lifting up the cross that hung around his neck to kiss it, "did not even relay those orders t' his officers. General Smith of the Eighteenth Corps said that he plain refused to obey. Every living soul left among the tatters of our three corps knew 'twas impossible. So, after issuing that madman's order two more times with not a man movin' forward so much as an inch, Bloody Grant saw 'twas either court-martial the whole army or pretend he'd never said such a thing. So here we are building better earthworks than those we scraped out with our blessed fingernails in that godforsaken attack. Here lads, let me put me shoulder t' that."

The sergeant stepped forward to help lift the log that Louis and Devlin had been trying to wedge into place atop their fortification. Flynn stepped back, dusted his hands, and nodded.

"Now take a moment t' catch yer breath, lads. Lord knows ye earned a bit of rest for all ye've been through."

Louis slumped down onto the ground.

Alive. And isn't that a miracle?

No less a miracle than that, though 3,000 had just died, not another man of his small circle had fallen. Others had died or were missing, men whose names and faces he had just begun to know. Better to try to forget them. In battle he'd stand shoulder to shoulder, even risk his life for any man in his company, but best not to hold the names of the new ones too close to his heart. Best not to make more friends. Better just to think of those remaining few who had begun this with him. Tired, worn out as old dishrags, but among the living. Sergeant Flynn and Corporal Hayes with their heads together talking. Songbird and Joker, Bull sitting across from him.

Louis met the eyes of each of his friends in turn, mouthing the words. *Thank you.*

Songbird nodded. Joker gave him a wry grin. Bull rolled his eyes up toward the sky as if to say only heaven knew how they'd made it this far.

Louis rested his face in his dirty, blistered hands. *The six of us might make it through this terrible war alive.*

For some reason, that thought brought tears to his eyes.

CHAPTER TWENTY-ONE
STALEMATE

Wednesday, June 8, 1864

"Sure and I've been here before."

Louis and Artis looked up from the circle they'd drawn in the dirt between them. Only three aggies remained inside. Each of the boys—for that was exactly how both of them had felt for the last half hour of their game, like boys again and not grim fighting men—had won exactly the same number of marbles. Each had managed to knock twenty of those little balls of chipped clay or agate out of the ring with their shooters.

"Where's that, you dumb Irishman?" Artis said in a pleasant voice. "At a cutthroat game of marbles?"

"No, ye ignorant savage," the scar-faced soldier answered in just as friendly a voice.

Francis O'Grady. That's the man's name.

Artis had introduced him to Louis as one of his best buddies and a faithful mess mate. Part of being friends with Artis meant enduring the sort of teasing that Indians often only reserved for each other. The two traded insults with each other the way other companions might pass the time of day or remark upon the weather. From what Artis had told Louis, O'Grady was always ready to share a spare blanket or whatever food was sent him from home, and to watch out for his mess mates on the battlefield. Though Louis could tell that O'Grady's singing was nowhere as sweet as Devlin's, he was quick to raise his voice in a song.

Francis O'Grady was the old man in Artis's company, having joined up a full two years before his Mohawk protégé. The scar that drew a puckered line from his right forehead down to his jaw line was the result of a wound the sardonic Irishman had suffered during the Virginia Campaign of 1863. O'Grady, Artis had explained, helped his Mohawk friend learn the little tricks of survival a rookie soldier needed to learn.

The fact that O'Grady was with them now was evidence of that. When the two of them had gone to search out a level place to play their game, O'Grady had come with them. Not to play, but to sit with his rifle in his arms on a fallen log. Although he looked relaxed, Louis noticed how O'Grady's eyes were never still. Even when he seemed to just be stretching he was actually looking around behind him. This close to the Rebel lines they might be taken unaware. So O'Grady was keeping guard.

"Where you been before, aside from dodging duty?" Artis said, taking aim at the red agate marble to the left.

Click!

Both his shooter and the red marble spun out of the circle.

O'Grady slapped the trunk of the oak tree beside him. "Here!" he said.

Artis nodded. "Oh, I see. So that's the tree that you and your other little monkey brothers and sisters was born in?"

Louis had a hard time keeping a straight face at that one. O'Grady's shoulders shook a bit as he lowered his head to cover the fact that he'd been tickled by Artis's barb. Apparently, Artis even amused himself with that one. His aim was off as he shot at the brown clay marble to the right.

It was Louis's turn now, but he waited to hear if O'Grady could match his Mohawk friend.

O'Grady shook his head sadly. "And here I thought I was talking to an eagle-eyed son of the forest and not a blind man." He cocked his head to stare at a spot on the tree's wide trunk.

"Well, I'll be a monkey's uncle," Artis said.

"No relative of mine." O'Grady grinned.

Louis walked over to look at the marks on the trunk he'd assumed to be nothing more than scars made by errant bits of iron or lead. Where battles had been fought it was hard to find a tree untouched by flying metal.

Louis traced the letters with his little finger.

FXO '63

"Francis Xavier O'Grady," Artis's mess mate said. "We took this very ground last year and then gave it up again. Most don't know we got this far, but there's me initials in the trunk to prove me claim."

O'Grady sighed.

"Go back to yer game, lads. I'm itching to see at least one clear-cut victory that doesn't end in a tactical withdrawal or a stalemate."

Stalemate. Both sides dug in and facing each other like two snapping turtles with their heads pulled into their cracked shells.

Although no shots came from the other side, Louis kept low as he walked back toward his own company. He did stop for a moment, though, where a merlon, a raised battlement with embrasures, gave a view of the no-man's-land between the two armies.

Free of the dead and dying for now, he thought, looking through the open spaces for shooting.

During the three days of battle, parts of the bloodied ground had been piled six deep with bodies. That many of them were not yet dead but only wounded had been no cause for hope. Anyone who ventured out on that field, whether for mercy or not, was a target. The fourth of June brought a halt to battle, but no truce.

Some said Lee himself refused a cease-fire for Union doctors to go out and minister to those men who were dying slowly, moaning and calling for water. Others said Grant wouldn't agree to the terms. Men in gray uniforms were also out there among the wounded, though nowhere near so many as blue-clad soldiers. Leaving them out there to die cut the diminishing Confederate forces just that much more.

Because generals refused to help the wounded didn't mean that the common soldiers couldn't try. When the dark of the first night came, Louis was among those who volunteered to crawl out and bring in the nearest of those so desperately hurt, they couldn't crawl to safety on their own.

It was hard work disentangling the living from the dead, but it was worth it to hear the two men Louis dragged back one after another weakly whisper their thanks. Whether they survived or not, he never knew, though their chances were slim. Both had so many grave wounds that likely more of their blood had soaked into the soil than still flowed through their veins.

June 5 passed and then June 6.

Anyone who tried to lift a head above the fortifications was soon driven back by fire from the other side. As the pitiless sun beat down, the cries of the wounded faded.

I'll hear those cries in my dreams. And then, even worse, I'll hear that silence.

On the fourth day, the seventh of June, an agreement was reached. Parties of stretcher bearers dashed into the field from North and South alike. Hundreds had been crying for aid just after the battle, but only two were found still living. Scant work for the doctors, but more than enough for those like Louis who volunteered to dig graves.

Louis turned from the vantage point over the deadly ground between the armies.

And now, to top it all off, our leaders are fighting each other.

Joker had passed on the latest gossip to him just that morning. Their own Union generals were now at bitter odds with each other.

It wasn't Grant's meat-grinder approach, using up men like cattle sent to the slaughter, that had stirred up opposition from the other top generals. Bloody Grant was getting more praise in the press than the rest of them. Getting good publicity meant almost as much as winning battles.

As Louis passed men who knew him, some raised a hand in tired greeting, but none said a howdy-do.

Too worn out to even talk.

Not just from the work, but from the blasted heat and the constant uncertainty.

No one ever knows what to expect next. And thinking of that, what the Sam Hill is happening now?

Ahead, men were standing up and pointing.

"Oh my Lord!" someone shouted from down the length of the trench, standing up and waving to Louis. It was Joker. Songbird and Bull were by his side. "Come see the circus what's come into town."

Louis quickened his pace to join them.

What's that heading our way? Oh my Lord, indeed!

A man seated backward on a mule was being led their way. A large placard was fastened to his chest. A drummer walking in front beat out the "Rogue's March" as the unfortunate rider was paraded through camp. Men were hooting and hollering. Some tossed clods of mud as the unfortunate man passed them.

"What's them signs say?" Bull asked. "I ain't got me spectacles."

Louis read the sign aloud.

"Libeler of the press."

"And what might that mean?" Songbird mused.

The officer holding the reins of the mule lifted his hand. The crowd quieted as he brandished a piece of paper.

"General Meade's proclamation. It reads, 'This reporter, one Edward Crapsey, the *Philadelphia Inquirer* correspondent, is to be put without the lines of this camp and not allowed to return for repeating base and wicked lies to the effect that only General Grant wanted to keep moving south and that General Meade was on the point of committing a blunder unwittingly.'"

The officer lowered his hand, the drummer began to beat out the march again, and the little procession continued on.

"Now there's the reason why General Meade will never be the president of this land," Kirk said.

"How's that?" Louis said.

Kirk pointed a finger toward the sky. "While we're fighting it out on these lines, Chief, our generals up there are already looking to what they'll do when the war is over. Every bit of fine publicity Grant gets puts him closer to that highest office. Being the winning general at Gettysburg, for a time the Old Snapping Turtle was the man of the hour. Now his star is falling while Bloody Grant's goes ever higher."

How, in the middle of a war, could a general think about becoming president?

Louis shook his own head to try to clear it.

"Now Meade's a gone goose for sure," Kirk continued, dropping his hand.

"How's that?" Devlin asked.

Kirk grinned. "Songbird, if your family was involved in politics like mine is back home in Albany, you'd understand that there's one enemy no one can ever defeat, even a major general who's been a hero of the republic. That enemy's not Robert E. Lee, but one a good deal nastier. The press. Mark my words, from this day on you'll never again read a good word about the old Snapping Turtle in any paper."

The procession was a good fifty yards away and had stopped once more for the proclamation to be read. Even at that distance, Louis could see the look on the mud-spattered reporter's face was more angry than humiliated.

"War is bloody," Kirk concluded, "but politics and reporters is worse."

CHAPTER TWENTY-TWO
THE INDIAN GENERAL

Thursday, June 9, 1864

What day is this? The ninth? Maybe the tenth?

When they weren't fighting, a day could drag on as if it were a week. Then there'd be a battle and nights and days would streak past fast as falling stars across the sky.

One thing for sure, it was near time to eat. Louis's stomach was telling him that. Back down the trench the cooking fire was going—fed by the rails they'd pulled from a fence back a hundred yards behind the fortifications. But first he was going to take his letter to the mail wagon.

One of the men by that cooking fire cleared his throat and

started to sing. Songbird, of course. As always, the tune he chose was one that fit what they all felt.

> *"Just before the battle, Mother,*
> *I am thinking most of you.*
> *While upon the field we're watching,*
> *with the enemy in view.*
> *Comrades brave are round me lying,*
> *filled with thoughts of home and God;*
> *For well they know that on the morrow,*
> *some will sleep beneath the sod."*

Mother.

He patted the breast pocket that held the letter from M'mere. The letter in his hand was his most recent letter to her. As in all the others he'd written, there was little about fighting and much about his friends, the food they ate, the land they marched through, the interesting people he met—like Artis Cook, who was walking along with him to send out a letter of his own

"Am I in that?" Artis pointed with his chin at the sealed letter in Louis's hand as they strolled toward the mail wagon. "You tell her about my trying to turn you into a civilized Indian like us Iroquois."

"As I recall, I told my mother that she was right about Mohawks being the ugliest Indians on the continent."

"Second-ugliest."

The two walked on a ways in silence.

"Bet you told her about us meeting the general," Artis said, his voice serious for a change.

Louis nodded. "He really is something special!"

"Wasn't it grand when he called the two of us over to him?" Artis said. His face was glowing now.

The two of them had been playing marbles again—Louis down by a dozen—when word reached them that none other than the Big Indian himself was inspecting their fortifications.

The Big Indian. That was what everyone called Brevet General Ely S. Parker, the broad-shouldered Seneca soldier who was the highest-ranking Indian in the whole Union army. He was a field engineer and reputed to be one of the best-educated men in the army. He was also Grant's close friend and personal secretary. And in addition to that, he was one Indian who truly could be called a chief. He'd been chosen by his Seneca people to be their Grand Sachem.

The marbles game was abandoned. The two of them headed to the easternmost fortifications where the general was rumored to be.

"From what I hear," Artis said as they made their way around a redoubt, "General Parker saved Grant and his staff from falling into an ambush back in the Wilderness. Grant was trying to check on the front but got lost in that tangle of roads and fallen trees. Parker was the only one who realized where they were. He turned their party around just as a Rebel company was about to close in and cut them off."

Artis was so busy telling his story that they almost stumbled down the embankment into the backs of a party of officers gathered on the lower side of the redoubt. None of them paid any notice to the two boys. They were listening too intently to the broad-shouldered officer with jet-black hair, neatly trimmed goatee and mustache who sat high on horseback before them.

"Another eighteen inches of soil should be added to those traverses," the brown-skinned man was saying, "if your intent is to defilade the interior space of your field works."

The Big Indian, for sure. No other high-ranking officer has a face like that. He surely does look like a chief too.

Finally, the engineers began to drift away now from the big man, their conference finished. General Parker sat there, as if lost in his thoughts.

"Think he feels as far away from home as we do?" Louis whispered to Artis.

General Parker turned his head slightly in their direction.

Eyes like a hawk's.

The shadow of a smile came to the Indian general's face. "Soldiers," he said, lifting one hand from the reins, "come on over here."

They were down the embankment in a flash.

"Yes, sir!" they said as one, snapping a salute to the mounted man.

And won't this be something to write home to M'mere about? An Indian general on a fine black horse passing the time of day with me?

The general looked down at them, the subtle smile still on

his face. Then he cleared his throat and focused his hawk eyes on Artis.

"*Skanoh,*" General Parker said.

"*Sehkon,*" Artis answered.

The general laughed out loud. "Hah! So you're a Mohawk, eh?"

"Yessir, been that way all my life." Artis grinned.

It wasn't the kind of remark Louis imagined most soldiers making to a superior officer, fellow Iroquois or not, but it seemed to tickle General Parker, as his smile broadened.

He turned slightly in his saddle to look down at Louis. The general's horse took a step closer to Louis and began nuzzling his shoulder the way most horses did whenever Louis was near. Louis stroked its nose.

The general chuckled and leaned forward to pat his horse's neck. "Found a new friend, have you, Midnight?" he said softly.

Then his voice deepened again. "Good with horses, are you?"

Louis wondered if he'd overstepped by being so familiar with the general's horse. He felt his ears redden.

"I . . . I suppose so, sir," he stammered, looking down.

"At ease, son." Out of the corner of his eye Louis saw the imposing man above him was studying his face. "Not Haudenosaunee, though. Not one of our longhouse people?"

"No sir, Abenaki."

"Ah, a people of great determination."

Those words, spoken with such warmth and certainty, removed any embarrassment Louis had been feeling. They needed no reply and so he didn't make one. He stood there, Artis by his left side, the general looking off in the distance, the three of them enjoying a companionable silence.

General Parker cleared his throat again.

"How old are you two boys?"

Artis answered first.

"Just gone eighteen," he said.

It never occurred to Louis to do anything but tell the plain truth. Plus that piece of paper in his shoe had worn out long ago.

"Fifteen, sir."

The look on General Parker's face changed a little then. It had been friendly before, but now there was something like tenderness in the way the dark-mustached man looked down and nodded.

"I thought as much. And I'll bet there's not a white man in this army who thought you less than seventeen."

"Suppose not," Louis said, looking up with a grin. General Parker lifted his right hand to tap the place where the brown skin of his own left wrist was exposed above the riding glove.

"It takes another Indian to know, doesn't it?"

"Yessir," Louis said, turning his eyes politely back down toward the ground.

Neither of them uttered a word beyond that, but to Louis that long moment of silence they shared was when they said the most to each other. It was not like with some white men who get nervous when you don't chatter like a jaybird.

General Parker took off his glove. He touched his right hand to his heart, then held that hand out to Louis, who took it in an Indian handshake. Their strong right hands together in a loose, relaxed way as strong as the flow of water. The general leaned farther over to shake with Artis.

"*Niaweh,*" Artis said.

The Indian general shook his head. "No, my boy. It is I who should thank you and your friend for your service. *Niaweh hah!*"

General Parker straightened, nodded one final time, and rode away.

A good thing to write to his mother about. In fact, it took up most of the two pages of paper that Louis had been able to scrounge. Paper was sometimes scarce as hen's teeth. Everyone who could manage to scribble a few words was writing home whenever they had a spare moment.

Must be ten tons of letters traveling between Virginia and the North every week.

And some back in the other direction too.

"Nolette, Louis," the man on the wagon called out. It surprised Louis so much that he couldn't answer.

"Here!" Artis shouted for him, before the mail clerk could put the letter away.

If it hadn't been for Artis, he might not even have gotten that letter. So Louis started reading the letter aloud to him as soon as he opened it. Once he'd started, though, it was too late to stop when it got embarrassing.

The handwriting was the same as before but this letter was more than twice as long. It began as it had before:

*Your Mama, she does miss you, my son.
I pray Bon Dieu that you be well.
I am glad you wrote to me and that you are
still alive and have not been hurt badly in
any way. You know that I, your mother, I
think of you always and I pray for you.*

Then more of her everyday voice crept in.

*I go to the Church and burn for you the
candles and also for the friends whose names
you have put on paper for my eyes.*

Louis sighed at the thought of those candles being lit, M'mere speaking the names of Artis and Sergeant Hayes and Corporal Flynn and each of his mess mates. Her strong prayers opening wings above their heads like protective angels.

The next lines made his heart rise up in his chest.

*What I tell you of now will make you
smile, I think. I have bought land for us. It
is good land and will grow good foods. Also*

there is woods. Many ash trees rise up from
their roots there to give themselves to us for to
make the baskets. I have found many good
medicine plants that tell me they will help
me with the healings. And there are fish in
the streams and good hunting is there also. It
will be a fine place for me, your mother, and
for the children you will have.

That was the first page. Louis almost did not turn to the second. But Artis, who was looking over his shoulder, nudged him hard in the back.

"Keep on. I want to know more about all them kids you are going to have."

Louis turned the page, took a breath and pressed on.

I have been speaking of you to the family
of Azonis. She and her Mama and Papa
and four brothers have now come down here to
make and sell the baskets, also beading. My
how she has grown up now, fine and strong,
yet she still holds you in her thought, my son.

His ears were burning, but Artis nudged him again.

"That's not the end of it," Artis said. "It's getting good."

Louis read on.

She is here beside me as I wrote. I show her how to make the strawberry basket. She now will add words. These are her words. Hello Louis. I hope you remember me. I look for you to come home.

That is all for now, my son. Your letters are in my heart. You will come home safe.

Your loving Mama

Sophie

Louis folded the pages back up and slipped them into the envelope. He unbuttoned his breast pocket, tucked the envelope in next to his mother's first letter, buttoned the pocket again.

"Who's Azonis?" Artis asked.

"A girl," Louis said in a grudging voice.

"Well, I hoped to God she wasn't a chicken," Artis chuckled. "Seeing as how your ma has you already married off to her and is counting on twelve grandchildren."

Louis spun toward Artis, his hands balled up into fists. "Don't you dare tell anyone about this!"

Artis stepped back, both hands raised with open palms.

"Whoa up, Louis. I won't breathe a word about it to a soul. You really like this girl, eh?"

The picture of Azonis Panadis's sweet young face looking over at him as they sat side by side in the Church of St. Ann filled Louis's memory. Her long black hair had fallen over one of her eyes, dark eyes that twinkled with mischief and intelligence. Their families had known each other forever. Sometimes they had traveled together and the father of Azonis had been one of his own father's closest friends.

Azonis.

They had played together when they were little children. Her ideas had always gotten him into trouble—like the time she decided they should dress their dogs up like people and one of M'mere's best blouses had ended up getting torn. He had always followed her, done whatever she told him to do. She was a year older than him, had been taller than him. Until this last year when he had grown to be as big as a man and he had noticed that when she looked at him she had to lift up her chin. And she had stopped telling him what to do. Instead she had begun looking at him as if she expected him to say something.

He had thought of her. And now he knew that she had been thinking of him.

She holds me in her memory.

Louis felt as if his feet were about to leave the ground.

"Yes," he said. "I really do like her."

179

By the time Louis got back, it was time to eat. He did so in a happy silence, but despite the fact that Louis's thoughts were on his memories of the face of Azonis Panadis, he still heard the feet quietly approaching him from behind.

Louis turned toward Sergeant Flynn before his name was spoken.

"Sir."

The burly sergeant shook his head. "There's no sneaking up on you, is there, me boy?"

"No, sir."

Flynn laughed.

"Good tidings, me boy. There's t' be no more attacking. We'll be falling back from the line."

CHAPTER TWENTY-THREE
ACROSS THE WIDE RIVER

Monday, June 13, 1864

No rest for the weary. We must of covered thirty miles since yesterday's sunset.

They might be falling back, but they were not retreating. Although they'd been through some of the worst fighting in the war and were all worn and tired to the bone, they'd been walking through the night. The Irish Brigade was to be part of yet another attempt to get around the defenses between them and Richmond.

The sun in the middle of the sky again, they finally stopped, allowed a few minutes to rest while some obstacle was cleared from the road ahead.

"Lads," Sergeant Flynn said, "gather here. It's some explanation ye deserve of what we're up t'. Even though we've seen the elephant, there's more ahead for us and it's toe the mark. Petersburg is where me betters say we're bound."

Flynn picked up a stick and made two lines in the soft ground.

"Now here's us, the Army of the Potomac. And here's dear old General Lee and his boys hunkering down, 'n' expecting another frontal attack."

Flynn chuckled, though there was not much humor in it, as he drew a long arrow leading back and around.

"But here's us now. One hundred thousand men tippy-toeing away and not a Rebel aware they're facin' empty trenches. Sure and it'll be another day before they discover we've moved to come at Richmond from below and behind."

Flynn scraped a curving line and jabbed in the point of the stick. "Crossing here."

"The James River?" Corporal Hayes asked.

From the tone of his voice, he doesn't sound much interested.

"Aye. They're putting in a great pontoon bridge t' bring across the horses and mules and the heavy artillery and the wagons. But the river is wide. It'll take at least a day or two to get that bridge built. And since there's not a Moses among us to part the waters, the Second Corps, all twenty-two thousand strong, including us fine fighters of the Sixty-ninth, will be floatin' over first by ferry boats."

Is that a river or an ocean?

The broad expanse of water that shone below them looked to be a mile wide. The light of a sun soon to set beyond the far side danced on the top of big waves.

How can anyone throw a bridge across that?

There was feverish activity on the near bank. Engineers were assembling pontoons and stacking great loads of planks on flatboats.

"Two miles down from here," Flynn said, coming up on Louis's right, "that's where the river narrows to a mere half mile. Ye might find it hard to envision, but for certain sure they're going to span the James."

Wish I could see that bridge when it's done. It'll be a wonder, for sure.

Gunports and transport barges were being pulled up to the landing below them. The engineers and navy boys on board all stared at the men of the 69th as they marched by.

"What are them popinjays in their pretty blue uniforms googling their eyes at?" Belaney muttered.

"They're just admiring our fine duds," Kirk said, "and wondering where they might find clothes so well decorated with sweat and mud and dust and blood as ours."

Louis glanced down at the tattered sleeves of his coat, the holes in the knees of his pants, his boots stained red from Southern mud and dust.

We're a regiment of scarecrows compared to them with their pressed pants and coats and their clean faces. But would they look as good if they'd just been fighting and marching and sleeping in the dirt like us for the last six weeks?

Soon they were on the bobbing deck of the first of the transport ships.

"Been on the water before?" Songbird asked.

"Some," Louis answered. "But never in a boat the size of a house."

"Twice as big as any house I ever lived in," Kirk said, leaning over the rail.

How can something as large as this float? Listen to how them planks thump under our feet. Almost like a drum. Won't this be something to write M'mere and Azonis about?

By dawn of the next day, they were all across and assembled at Windmill Point. But the expected order to move out hadn't come. The sun now stood two hands high above the horizon. Sergeant Flynn, who had gone off to find out what the delay was, was just returning.

"Sergeant, sir," Kirk said, "have the officers finished having their breakfast yet? Or will we be waiting till they've had dinner?"

Flynn shook his head in disgust. "Our orders now are for the whole of Second Corps t' sit and wait for the arrival of sixty thousand rations from General Butler that we're to carry with us to Petersburg."

"Hurry up and wait," Louis said, surprising himself by speaking his thoughts aloud.

The other men chuckled at his words, but Flynn's face stayed grim.

"I'll wager you boys a dollar against a donut," Sergeant Flynn growled, "that them rations never do get here. But there's no point t' complaining. For it's the joy of me life that when things go wrong in this army, with the fine generals we have leading us, they kin always go worse."

Flynn's words were a prophecy. By midmorning, when no rations had arrived, a disgusted General Hancock decided they'd waited long enough. They set out on what was supposed to be a sixteen-mile march to Petersburg to join the 16,000 men of General Smith's Corps who had crossed the Appomattox River to the west and would reach Petersburg first.

The sun lifted to the middle of the sky, moved a hand's width across and then another hand's width down.

Mid-afternoon. We've gone more than just sixteen miles, what with changing directions on these roads that wind in and out like a nest of snakes.

March and countermarch. Toward the sunset, then away from it.

Thunder? No. Batteries of artillery letting loose somewhere miles ahead of us.

Through some trick of the land or the atmosphere, though, the far-off thud and crackle of cannons and muskets came and went. First from one direction and then another—even when they stood still while the leaders of the march studied their maps and cussed. It left Louis wondering if the battle sounds were real or only imagined by his mind, which was about as worn out as his body.

Finally, when the hand of darkness spread over the land, a halt was called. Exhausted men who'd now walked for the better part of two days slumped to the ground. Louis lifted his head—which took some effort—to look around the ranks of dusty soldiers and pick out his friends. Torches flickered here and there, but were hardly necessary. The moon was so bright, it cast faint shadows on the ground.

There Kirk and Devlin were, a few yards away leaning back to back, too tired to crack a joke or sing a note. Bull lay on his side next to them, worn out past complaining. And there was Corporal Hayes, sitting on a dead tree, staring at his boots. Sergeant Flynn was nowhere in sight. Louis closed his eyes.

Suddenly Flynn's voice boomed out near him and he jerked awake.

"Boys," Sergeant Flynn said, his voice even more disgusted than usual, "I'm back from getting the lay of the land. And here's the grand news. We're no more than an hour's march from Petersburg. A sergeant friend who's just come as a courier from near the front with Hancock tells me that our major general has vowed t' shoot the next mapmaker he sees. The lovely directions we was given had us following roads what don't exist t' a destination well within the enemy lines. Our dear little map might have been drawn by General Robert E. Lee himself. By my calculations we just marched thirty-two miles t' get to a place sixteen miles away and we're not there yet. The only good news is that the courier knows the way back t' Petersburg, so we'll not get lost goin' there."

Flynn paused, but Louis could tell he wasn't done yet from the look on his face.

"It gets better, doesn't it?" Corporal Hayes asked.

"Ye might say. It seems our Second Corps was expected t' take part in the assault on the Rebel lines. Unbeknownst to any of us from General Hancock on down! And why did we not know that? Because our beloved Lieutenant General Ulysses S. Grant, bless his heart, never saw fit t' mention that t' any of us, from the Snapping Turtle on down to our own General Winfield S. Hancock. In any event, that assault, t' the surprise of all, actually met with some success. So General Smith decided it would be unfair to the poor dear Rebels to press the advantage by chasing them further."

"General Smith stopped the attack when he was winning?" Corporal Hayes said.

"Bless his heart," Flynn replied. "Givin' the Johnnies time to regroup and reinforce. And now we're t' take part in a night assault on the great line around the city. No more than ten miles of forts and batteries and breastworks."

"Oh Lord!" Hayes said.

For once there was not the hint of a question in his voice.

"Indeed," Sergeant Flynn replied.

CHAPTER TWENTY-FOUR

THE UNITED STATES
COLORED TROOPS

Thursday, June 16, 1864

Just like always, things are not going as planned.

As soon as they arrived, the Second Corps was sent in to take the place that had been held by Brigadier General Hincks and the USCT of the Eighteenth Corps.

The USCT. That stood for the United States Colored Troops. The Eighteenth was one of the Union Army's new regiments of Negro troops, most of whom had been slaves. Some had questioned whether men of color had the intelligence or courage to be good soldiers. But the black men in blue had led the first assault the prior evening with great valor. They'd overwhelmed the Confederate defenses before being ordered to reluctantly fall back and wait for Second Corps to renew the assault.

But no order to attack was given. The night had passed, and the whole morning of the next day.

As Louis checked his rifle and counted his cartridges yet again, he saw the shadow of a familiar presence moving up behind him.

"Yes, sir, sergeant," he said without looking up.

"Nolette," Flynn chuckled. "I'm sending ye off on a difficult and dangerous mission. One of me friends told me the commissary wagon has actually brought up some fresh fruit and vegetables. It'll be yer job t' bring back as much as ye kin of them rare delicacies."

No attack?

Louis didn't ask that question out loud, but Flynn read it from his face.

"There'll be a day or more before we take t' the field again," Flynn said. "That long march took more of a toll on our good General Hancock than it did on us. The great wound in his thigh he suffered at Gettysburg opened again. The poor man is sloughing out bits of bone. And so, Saints preserve us, the decision t' attack or not rests alone on the shoulders of Old Baldy." Flynn snuffed. "Our dear General Smith, who doubts that even the forty thousand good men in blue we've now gathered will be enough t' breach the Rebel works."

Bon Dieu help us.

The commissary wagons were just beyond the bivouac of the Eighteenth Corps. As Louis made his way, two empty sacks over his shoulder, he thought about the formidable fortifications they'd sooner or later be attacking

The Dimmock Line.

That was what the great ring of defense erected around the strategic railhead of Petersburg had been named—for the Southern engineer who'd designed it. The walls and trenches that had stopped them at Cold Harbor had been constructed in only a matter of days. The Dimmock Line had been more than two years in the building.

Louis passed an awed group of Union engineers discussing the palisades, abatis, bombproofs, and redoubts that lay ahead of them.

"No less than fifty-five separate redans," an engineer lieutenant with blond muttonchops was saying.

Redans, that'd be those thick-walled little forts along the length of the line, each one bristling like an angry porcupine with cannons for quills.

As Louis continued on he realized that he was tapping his fingers on his ammunition pouch, keeping time to a song. It was coming from somewhere nearby—deep, melodic voices accompanied by hand-clapping.

> *"Ain't gonna turn around*
> *Ain't gonna turn around*

We gonna take that ground
We gonna take that ground"

A group of twenty or more black soldiers making that music were there sitting on the grass. No doubt they'd been among the ones in the thick of battle the day before. Most had bandages wrapped around their limbs or their heads. But they were smiling as they sang.

"Soldier," a voice with a heavy Southern accent called to him, "y'all one of us'ns?"

Louis turned to see not a Confederate, but a man in a uniform bluer and newer than his own. The man's inquisitive smile shone from a young, friendly face only a shade darker than his own. Seeing how dark his own skin was, even browner now from sunburn and dirt, the man had mistaken Louis for a mulatto.

"Nope," Louis said, reaching out to shake the Negro soldier's hand, "Indian. Louis Nolette, Company E of the Sixty-ninth."

"Indian?" the young man said in a delighted voice, pumping Louis's hand. "A real Indian! My, oh my! My old granny, she is a Indian herself. Has them long braids and high cheekbones. Chickahominy from right roun' these parts. She still livin' in Petersburg, y'know. Matter of fact, I thought I'd be payin' her a call just yesterday. And we would of done so if they hadn't of called us back. Me and the boys in muh company, we had such a head of steam up that we was on our way to Richmond to tie a knot in old Jeff Davis's tail. But I am forgettin' muh manners. Private First Class Thomas Jefferson, of the Virginia Jeffersons and Tenth U.S. Colored of the Eighteenth."

"Pleased," Louis said. He liked the warm, rich voice and the demeanor of Private Thomas Jefferson. Self-confident with a sense of humor. He was as tall and broad-shouldered as Louis. Despite his dark skin, though, the man's patrician features were more like those of a white man.

Jefferson? Does that mean . . . ?

"Now you might be wonderin'," Private Jefferson continued, guessing the question that was forming in Louis's mind, "about muh name. I 'spect you might be thinkin' I'm fixin' to claim that one of the Foundin' Fathers of this fine nation was muh great-grandfather." Jefferson chuckled. "Well, sir, I am not. Nossir, not at all. Massah Tom's brother was a little faster getting to the slave quarters that night. So I can only claim President Thomas Jefferson as muh uncle."

Louis smiled.

Private Jefferson had not yet let go of Louis's hand. "Now, what was it you said your name was, sir?"

"Louis Nolette, just Louis."

"Louis, my friends call me just Jeff, seeing as how Mr. President is such a mouthful."

Louis's smile turned into a grin. "Like to walk with me for a spell, Jeff?"

"Muh pleasure, Louis."

As the two young men strolled through the camp, Jeff kept talking. Before long, they joined the long line of soldiers in front of the commissary wagons. As they inched their way forward, Louis's listening drew out the story of the previous day's battle and the fortifications that faced them.

"Now that line of forts there," Jeff said, one hand on Louis's shoulder as he pointed toward the west, "you know who did mos' uh thuh buildin' of them? Me and about two thousand other men wid skins as black as mine. A year ago, thas where ah was, breakin' my back wid a pick and shovel. Whilst Captain Dimmock was givin' high and mighty orders about what to put here and what to move there to make that line of his im-pregnable."

Jeff held out his broad right hand palm up and used the index finger of his left to trace a shape. "Fifty-five artillery batteries along a ten-mile stretch. Fum here to here. And ever' one of um set up like its own little fort with them twenty-four-pounder siege guns. So me and mos' of thuh other men in muh company, all being fum aroun' here before we all decided to take French leave and put on this fine blue uniform, we knows jus' where to go when they sets us to fighting. We knows evah weak spot, evah ditch. Fust thing we does, we takes to this ravine between batteries Seven and Eight."

Jeff traced one of the lines in his palm. "And where did that come out? Right behind battery Nine, which we took without hardly a shot."

Their two hour assault had been so fierce that the U.S. Colored Troops of the Eighteenth took no fewer than five of the seven batteries captured that evening by the Union. Despite

Jeff's modest words about how easy it had been, Louis had already heard that the Colored Troops had encountered more than a little resistance. Their own casualties had been over 150 men as they rolled back an entire mile of the Dimmock Line.

Jeff chuckled. "They was running like chickens fum a fox," he said. "'N' well they might. When you's a boy in gray and you sees a bunch a' angry black men wid guns and bayonets comin' at you yellin' 'Remember Fort Pillow!' well, you better take to your heels!"

Fort Pillow, Tennessee.

Louis had read the newspaper stories about what happened there just three months ago. Rebel General Nathan Bedford Forrest, said to hate freed Negroes more than any other man in Dixie, had captured that fort along the Mississippi River. Of the 570 troops in the federal garrison, 262 had been Negro soldiers.

The Union commander of the fort, seeing how outnumbered they were, had surrendered almost at once. But then, either at Forrest's orders or because he turned a blind eye, the Rebel soldiers had begun shooting down unarmed black men with their hands raised. The final toll at Fort Pillow had been 231 Union dead—most of them black.

"Before we went into battle," Jeff said, his voice a reverent whisper now, "we all knelt down and took us a holy vow. Alluhs remembah Fort Pillow."

Louis nodded. "I understand."

As much as he'd grown to hate this war, Louis found himself

remembering again one of the reasons he had been willing to volunteer. The best reason of all.

No human being should ever own another person.

Jeff slapped his palms together as if killing a mosquito. "'N' then, when we had 'em running, they called us off. We could of kep' goin' and taken that whole line. Why'd they go and do that? Didn't they want us black men to win their war for um? We could see those Rebs didn't have even half what they needed to defend against us. We could see down the line that there was batteries just standin' empty but they wouldn't let us take um!"

He pointed again toward the Dimmock Line. "You know what they's doin' now over there? They's rushin' in men by that Norfolk and Petersburg rail line, reinforcin' what was weak. By the next time our generals finally gets up the nerve for anuddah attack, those Rebs is goin' to be ready. Where that line was made uh sand last night, tomorrow it is goin' to be iron. I do pity the next soldiers on our side who are goin' up agin' that line. They goin' to be cut to ribbons."

And those next soldiers sent against that line, those'll be us.

CHAPTER TWENTY-FIVE

ATTACK AT ALL HAZARDS

Saturday, June 18, 1864

"Men," Sergeant Flynn said, "Corporal Hayes and I have one command we'd like ye to be listenin' for. Corporal?"

"Down!" Hayes yelled.

Louis and all of the other men of E Company, veterans and new faces alike, dropped as one onto their bellies.

"Fine," Flynn said. "Ye can hop back up again, me lovelies. But don't be getting up till ye hear me or the corporal ask ye to do so. If ye hear the bugle blowin' the attack, stay where ye are. Even if ye have some fine big officer with all sorts of bars and braids on his clean blue uniform hollerin' at ye from back behind the parapet, pay the man no heed. And when yer down there don't be lifting up and looking about. Just roll to yer backs if you need to reload. That way ye might come out of this blessed thing with all the limbs and heads the good Lord saw fit to give us."

Two more days had passed without a major federal assault on the Dimmock Line. Now it was the afternoon of June 18.

The whole of Meade's mighty Army of the Potomac, 100,000 strong, was just sitting back on its haunches like a balky mule refusing to pull the plow no matter how hard its master whipped it with the reins and hollered giddyup.

Even a common private like me can see clear as spring water that we're stalled.

The federal generals, it seemed, could not get together on anything.

Burnside and his Ninth Corps wanted to attack one minute and not the next.

Birney, as the newest commander of all, was waiting for others to decide.

Hancock was still out of action with his old wound bleeding.

And the most hesitant of all was Old Baldy Smith. He'd believed for so long the false rumors that large numbers had reinforced the Rebel trenches that by now they were likely true.

To put it plain, everyone from the top down was remembering just one thing. Cold Harbor.

No wonder Sergeant Flynn is shaking his head at the foolishness of it. We milled around like a herd of sheep while those Rebels had time to get ready to give us a hot welcome. It's like waiting all spring and summer to plant a crop and not deciding to put it in till it's time for first frost.

Just yesterday, Joker had expressed it well. "You might say that our Grand Army of the Republic appears to of been infected by politeness. You attack first, General Burnside. Oh no, after you, General Smith, I insist. Like a bunch of naughty schoolboys, not wanting to be the first through the schoolhouse door to get paddled."

But not today, Louis thought. The Snapping Turtle finally had enough. Meade's orders left no doubt about what was to be done.

Flynn had shared the gist of the orders with them.

" 'Findin' it impossible to effect cooperation by appointing an hour for attack,' says the major general's order, 'I have sent a message t' each field commander to attack at all hazards and without reference t' each other.' "

Flynn looked at the men in the company. Then lifting his hands up as if holding a piece of paper between them, he mimed the gesture of crumpling that paper between his palms and tossing it over his shoulder.

"Forward march."

With Devlin to his left, Kirk to his right, and Belaney just behind him, Louis started to walk, one of thousands of anxious men.

I wonder where Artis is. Somewhere off there to the side of us, where the Legion flags are flying? Great Creator, watch over me and my friends.

As they passed the artillery batteries, a few of the cannoneers shouted "Huzzah!" and took off their hats. Most, though, stood silent or shook their heads at the thought of what lay ahead for the dumb infantrymen.

"You fixing to charge them works?" a crew member holding a rammer called to them.

"Nossir," Joker answered back. "Our plan's to start at a trot, turn, and head back at full gallop. We had enough of earthworks at the Bloody Angle and Cold Harbor."

Joker's voice was loud enough for their officers to hear, but not a one of them turned a head in his direction or said a word.

Louis looked up at the clear sky. From where the sun stood it was about four p.m. They were still on the safe side of the federal earthworks. Major General Birney was out in front of them now, telling the officers how to mass the brigade for its attack on the Rebel center.

We're too late and we all know it, Louis thought, glancing at the grim faces around him. *Three days ago, we might've pushed through all the way to Richmond. Now there's been time for the Confederates to bring up enough men to turn the field ahead into a killing ground.*

Four lines. The first two, where the men of the Irish Brigade were placed, was made up of veteran units. The two behind were the First Maine and the First Massachusetts. Heavy artillery regiments converted into infantry to make up for the immense losses of the past weeks.

Men who've not seen this sort of fighting before.

"Lads," Sergeant Flynn growled as he walked backward in front of their line, "soon as yer over the top, ye know what to do. Then wait for my command!" Sergeant Flynn looked over at Corporal Hayes. There was no expression on Hayes's face, but he nodded quicker than usual in agreement with the sergeant's words.

"Over the top, men!"

Louis wasn't sure which of the saber-waving officers gave that command, but all of E Company followed it without hesitating. Though when they reached the top of their works they all dove to their stomachs with such speed that they looked more like a great line of swimmers than an attacking army. A few shots popped from the Rebel line. Then it was quiet. No further response from the soldiers in gray a hundred yards away.

Those in back of us might figure this is going to be easy. But those Rebs are just waiting for better targets.

Louis knew now what every veteran learned. A man on his stomach is seldom hit by musket fire. Just like the Union boys, Southern soldiers tended to shoot high. For every minié ball with your name on it, a hundred pounds of lead whizzed over your head. So, as he crawled forward, he kept so low that he could taste dirt on his lips.

Still no Rebel fire.

The heavy breathing of other men around him as they crawled, the scrape of elbows and knees against hot red soil, the occasional soft curse as a man scraped a wrist or banged a knee on a stone. Farther from the safety of their own entrenchments. Closer and closer to the Reb earthworks.

A little stir went down the ranks, like hair standing up on the back of the neck of a giant. Louis turned his head.

A young lieutenant in a clean uniform ten yards away was waving his dang saber.

"Rise and charge!" the lieutenant was shouting.

Other officers began standing up, echoing his command.

"Rise and charge!"

Louis looked toward Sergeant Flynn, ten feet ahead. Low on his belly as the enlisted men around him their sergeant stayed still as a stone. So did Louis and the other common soldiers in the two lines of veterans.

Bravery was one thing. Plain suicide was another.

Sounds from behind him. He squirmed around to see what was going on. The third line, the men of the First Massachusetts were rising to their feet. Before they got halfway to their knees, hundreds of veterans between them and the enemy called back to them.

"Get back down, y' dang fools!"

"Y' can't take them works!"

"Lay down!"

"Down!"

Louis saw the looks on those Bay Stater faces as they realized the men shouting back over their shoulders at them were the Fighting Sixty-ninth, the bravest brigade in the army. As one, the First Massachusetts flopped back down and hugged the ground.

But now the First Maine stood up. The 850 men of that brigade figured they were made of tougher stuff. They began to march forward, ignoring the veterans' warnings, stepping over the prone figures of the three ranks ahead of them. One heavy-footed Mainer with a beard yellow as straw stepped right on Louis's back.

Louis paid it as little mind as he did the words some of those rugged Maine boys growled down at them.

"What's wrong with you Irish?"

"You a bunch of sissies?"

"Ain't you gonna fight like men?"

Then the First Maine was past them, moving on the double against the impregnable line ahead. Five, ten, fifteen yards away.

"May the good Lord who looks after fools and children protect 'em," Flynn said in a voice like that of an Old Testament prophet.

Louis closed his eyes.

But not soon enough. He saw the great burst of smoke and flame that billowed out of the thousands of rifle slots in the high earthworks as the Confederates opened fire en masse.

Not one man of the First Maine reached the Rebel lines. Less than a quarter were able to return.

Six hundred sacrificed like lambs, Louis thought as he wormed his way backward, pulling with him the weeping Maine boy who'd managed to stagger back and then fall by his side. *If we'd all charged, it would have been four times as many.*

No second attack went forward.

"Would you like to know the tally, lads?" Sergeant Flynn said in a weary voice the next morning. "A friend of mine at headquarters who keeps accounts of such matters, says there's been seventy-two thousand of us killed, wounded, or captured since we started in the Wilderness."

We've lost more men in the three months I've been a soldier than old Lee has in his whole army.

"But there's t' be no more attacks. Grant himself has agreed it's time t' rest and use the spade fer protection." Sergeant Flynn made a low sad sound like a growl from the back of his throat. "And a welcome change that'll be, if indeed we kin believe it t' be so."

CHAPTER TWENTY-SIX

A VISIT TO THE LINES

Monday, June 20, 1864

"If it han't been for them thirsty hosses, we woulda been in Petersburg now."

"Do tell," Artis said.

Louis looked up from the stump where he was sitting and whittling. He was trying to pull the shape of a bear out of the piece of pine Artis had picked up as he and Louis and their new friend, Private Thomas Jefferson, strolled among the stumps on the hill behind the USCT entrenchments.

"This used to be a forest," Artis said, flipping the piece of pine branch to him. "See what you can make of it now."

Precious little forest left around here. The Rebs had cleared most of it away for fortifications and to open a clear line of fire to the east. But the stumps at the edge of this stand of pines were just right for sitting.

The sky was as blue and clear above them as the firmament in the paintings Louis remembered from Father Andre's residence at St. Francis. There'd been peace in the blue skies of those paintings, blue that framed the figure of Jesus Christ lifting a hand in benediction. But when Louis looked up at that cloudless sky above them he just couldn't feel that sort of peace—not after all they'd been through.

Yesterday had been a Sunday that almost felt like Sunday. No fighting at all. Not even the drilling supposed to take place when there was no other action. On either side of the two opposing lines of dug-in trenches, redans, and fortifications, religious services had been held. The morning air had been hot, but so clear that the men of E Company could hear the hymns rising up from the other side.

Songbird Devlin cocked his head. "'Rock of Ages.' Not badly sung, but they could use a few baritones." He nodded. Then he reached into his coat and pulled out a pocket-sized book with a water-stained cover. "It's glad I am they're singing the good old hymns, and not these."

Louis leaned over to read the cover.

Hymns for the Camp. Published by the South Carolina Tract Society.

Songbird flipped through the pages. "Picked this up in one

of the trenches where some Johnny dropped it as he was skedaddling. Here's one to be sung to the tune of 'God Save the King.'

> "*Our loved Confederacy*
> *May God remember thee*
> *And Warfare stay;*
> *May he lift up his hand*
> *And smite the oppressor's hand*
> *While our true patriots stand*
> *With bravery.*"

Songbird shook his head. "It's a poor poet can't find a better rhyme for *hand* than the selfsame word. Ah, but hear what they're giving us now."

Louis and the others in their company listened. As sweet a version of "Amazing Grace" as he'd ever heard came floating to them light as the wings of a dove. Then, up and down the line of trenches, Union men began to join in until at least a thousand voices and hearts of men in both blue and gray were lifted above the earthly battlefield by a song.

Today, though, was Monday. Up at five a.m. with the bugle, drill and march till breakfast, drill and march again till the noonday meal. Then they were gathered together by Sergeant Flynn.

"We're to move again tomorrow," Flynn said, using a stick to sketch yet another plan just as smart as the dirt it was drawn in. "Our Second Corps and General Wright's just-arrived Sixth Corps. Sidesteppin' west, toward the Appomatox River t' cut the Weldon and Petersburg railway line that connects Petersburg with North Carolina."

A few heads nodded, but mostly the men just listened. Flynn handed Louis a paper. "Take this to headquarters."

It had been some sort of message from their new lieutenant. That job done, Louis had let his steps lead him first past Artis's nearby encampment, where he'd collected his friend. Then farther down the line by the bivouac of the Eighteenth Corps they'd found Jeff just as ready to waste some time.

Seeing how they took to one another, Louis used every spare moment to get the three of them together. Sometimes it was to play marbles—which Artis always won. Or they'd wrestle. Artis and Jeff were evenly matched there, but neither had been able to throw Louis. Other times, they'd just talk. Or, more accurately, Artis and Louis would listen to Jeff hold forth. His plan after the war was to become a preacher.

Makes sense. Never heard a better talker. Not even Father Andre.

So here they were, Artis half asleep in the sun, Louis whittling, Jeff speechifying from the pulpit of a pine stump about what might have been had certain white officers been as sharp as the black men they led.

"Yessuh," Jeff repeated, "them thirsty hosses." He paused, waiting.

"What horses?" Louis asked.

"The ones what pulls the artillery carriages," Jeff replied. "We was all set to move out towards them Rebs three hours before they let us go. But some officer misremembered that hosses needs to drink. Then when they finally saw how thirsty them hosses was, they unhitched um from the wagons and took um down to the river. And that was when we was supposed to be attackin.' Had to wait a good two hours whilst they got them hosses back in their traces."

"What's that?" Artis said.

Louis shaded his eyes with one hand as he closed the jackknife against his leg with the other. Some kind of commotion was going on in the camp below them. People were circling around a small group of men on horseback. The tallest rider was the Big Indian himself, General Parker. But the other two men, one of whom was a bearded civilian in a dark suit, were unfamiliar to him.

Jeff followed Louis's glance.

"Mah Lord," he exclaimed, standing up, brushing off the seat of his pants, and throwing on his jacket. "You know who that is?"

"The Big Indian," Louis said.

"General Ely Parker, one of my people," Artis added with a grin.

"No, next to him. That's the man hisself. Old Father Abraham."

Jeff started down the hill at a trot with Louis and Artis close behind him.

The President of the United States. Abraham Lincoln. My stars!

By the time they reached the expanding circle of the Colored Troops gathered around the three mounted men, Louis recognized who the third person on horseback, a man much smaller than the other two, had to be. Although he was suited up in the uniform of a common soldier and not the resplendent finery some officers wore, the stars on his shoulders showed that he was none other than Lieutenant General Ulysses S. Grant.

As Louis and Artis approached, General Parker's eyes caught theirs. He nodded to each of them in turn. Just one Indian to another. No one else in the crowd noticed it, not even Jeff, who was right by Louis's side. Every other face in the crowd was fixed on the person in the black suit.

Dressed like a boss undertaker, though he does look to be easy in the saddle. Not handling his horse like a city slicker.

The lanky, bearded man took off his hat and circled with it toward the sea of dark faces, using his reins to gently turn the horse he rode so that he presented that gesture to every face looking up at him. A loud cheer rose up through the crowd.

"We's with you, Mistah President," someone yelled.

"God bless you, suh!" Jeff shouted, waving both hands above his head.

Men began reaching their hands up to gently touch his horse or the hem of his coat, then pull their hands back to press them to their mouths or their hearts. Everyone was smiling, but there were tears in many eyes, including those of President Abraham Lincoln himself.

There's a man who cares for the folks around him. Or at least he knows how to make himself look like a man who cares.

Lincoln held up his hand. Silence came as quick as a heartbeat. Everyone waited for words from the Great Emancipator.

"Men," Lincoln said in a rough, choked voice. "Men of the Eighteenth, I . . ." His voice broke and he paused to take a breath. "Men," he continued, "for that is what you truly are. Thank you for your cheers, even though I am not worthy of them. I should be cheering for you, for your courage and your sacrifices. I promise you this. We accepted this war as a worthy object, and this war will not end until that object is attained. Under God, I will not rest until that time."

Virtually unnoticed as he sat his horse a few yards back from the swirl of admiring former slaves and free men, General Grant nodded at the president's words.

Louis saw that nod and the determined look on Grant's face.

Am I right about what I think I read from that look?

Louis looked over at Artis, who raised an eyebrow and nodded back at him. *You got it right.*

The inspired Negro soldiers around them were cheering even louder now, but Louis hardly heard them. A knot the size of a fist formed in his stomach.

Mon Dieu! Grant, he's going to send us back on the attack!

CHAPTER TWENTY-SEVEN
ONE MORE THRUST

Thursday, June 23, 1864

The thump of cannon, the crackling of muskets, the shouts and screams and confusion were behind him. Hard as that was to believe.

And I'm alive, Louis thought, looking at his blackened hands. His knee ached from running into something, there was a new tear in his shirt, his right hand was bleeding and he couldn't recall exactly what had caused any of that.

A sound came from the tent behind him. Songbird. But the only song that was issuing from his lips right now was a soft snore from the cot where he lay fully clothed, despite the heat. After stumbling back into camp from the futile Union attack, he'd been too tired to even take off his boots and his coat.

I'm bone-weary too, but I can't sleep.

Louis wiped some of the dirt and gunpowder stains off onto his pants.

Give thanks, his mother's remembered voice spoke in the back of his head.

"Bon Dieu, for preserving my friends yet again, *ktsi oleohneh.* Great thanks."

He plucked another briar from the torn cuff of his trousers. Then, picking up a stick, he began to draw in the dirt the way he'd seen Sergeant Flynn do so many times.

Here's our Second Corps, Louis thought, drawing three short lines in a row to stand for the Union divisions. He drew three more short lines below and behind them. *And here's Wright's corps just arrived.*

With the point of his stick Louis scratched two arrows, one for each of the corps, pointing toward the west. *And there's the way we was supposed to go to cut the Weldon rail line.* Nothing to it. Just cross the Jerusalem Plank Road and go two more miles west.

Louis shook his head. That had been the plan. But, as always seemed to be the case with everything in this campaign, things had gone wrong.

As they marched through the darkness and crossed the Jerusalem Plank Road, they found themselves in the sort of unpleasantly familiar tangle of woods and brush that E Company had encountered time and again since the Wilderness.

Good ground to hunt in for a man who knows it. Bad for keeping an army together.

Within a hundred yards Wright's corps lost contact with Birney's.

Louis drew a third arrow coming from the west.

And here comes Rebel General A. P. Hill and his men. Hitting right in between our two separated Union commanders, holding off Wright with one division and mauling us with the other.

The only thing they'd been able to do was retreat. And even that had been bungled. Not that many killed or wounded, but so many cut off and caught. A whole Union battery—six cannons and all their crew. Hundreds and hundreds of soldiers so beat down by weeks of battle that they just threw down their rifles and raised up their hands.

Louis thanked his lucky stars for his good night vision and always being able to remember ground he'd crossed. He'd helped E Company get back through the woods in a fighting retreat, kept their battle flag from being taken.

That, at least, is something we can be proud about.

No flag of the 69th had ever been lost to the enemy, right on down to this last battle. According to Flynn, no other regiment of men in blue could make that claim.

Louis thought about those who had been taken along with their flags. Seventeen hundred of the Second Corps now on their way to Andersonville, the Rebel prison that was one step lower than Hades.

I don't think I could stand that.

Being captured worried him more than being a casualty. According to last week's newspapers, that prison camp down in Georgia held more than thirty thousand men penned like hogs. The only two ways out were escape or death. Lots of ways to die there, too—starvation, sickness, getting beaten to death or shot by the guards.

Back at the start of this war, Louis knew, when one side captured a man from the other side, they'd just ask him to promise not to do any more fighting and then let him go. That hadn't worked so well, seeing as how the Union found itself capturing the same men again and again. Then they tried prisoner exchanges. That meant if you got caught, you'd be treated pretty well, since you could be used to get back some of the other side's own boys.

Now those days are long past.

No more prisoner exchanges.

The North can afford to lose more men than the South. By keeping those Rebel boys in our own prison camps—like the one in Elmira—we're slowly draining them dry. No matter that our boys are rotting in Andersonville. Plus it's different now that we're throwing the Colored Troops against them. That's really made the Rebs mad. They catch a black soldier, the usual thing that they do is just kill him outright.

Louis scraped the point of his stick across the ground, wiping out the lines and arrows he'd drawn. No sense to it. No matter how many diagrams you drew, war was just plain crazy and nothing in it would ever be simple. Louis sighed. Too much thinking about it was just making it worse. All you could do was try your best and help the men closest to you.

Louis studied the position of the sun. A good hour left before they'd have to assemble for roll call. He could crawl back into the tent next to Songbird. But even that seemed like too much of an effort right now. He leaned his arms and head forward on his knees and closed his eyes.

Hope I don't dream.

And in what seemed no more than the time it took to close his eyes, a hand was shaking him. He looked up at Corporal Hayes. One of the corporal's eyes was closed, the ends of his mustache were singed, and the left side of his face was swollen and scratched.

That big tree limb that was knocked loose by a shell and fell on him during the retreat.

Despite the bruises, the impassive look on the corporal's face was gone.

"The sergeant wants to have a word with us all," Hayes said, pulling Louis to his feet. "And thanks again, Chief," the corporal added in a softer voice, patting him on the shoulder, "for lifting up that heavy tree limb. I would have been caught for sure by those Rebs who were on our tails."

"Wasn't nothing," Louis said, "sir."

"Lads," Sergeant Flynn said, "I'm glad t' see ye hale and hearty. But as ye know, the rest of our lads were not so lucky. There's so few of us left that our three New York Regiments, the Sixty-third, the Sixty-eighth, and our own Fightin' Sixty-ninth are bein' consolidated."

Flynn paused and as he did so Joker raised a bandaged hand.

"Sergeant, can you tell me what it means to be consolly-dated? Will it hurt much?"

It was a weak joke, but a few men still laughed. The laughter, though, quickly died away as the serious look stayed on their master sergeant's face.

"T' be consolidated means that our poor regiments have been so shot into pieces that"—he held up three fingers on his right hand and then grasped them with his left—"we'll all three be combined into one. Now, that's not such a bad thing, for our own Captain Richard Moroney of the Sixty-ninth is to be the man in command of the consolidated regiment. But that's not the whole of it. As you know, we lost Colonel Kelly, our commanding officer of the Second Corps, last Saturday. And we'll not see his like again for that cool courage and gentle manners and modesty and honesty of his that made us love him."

Flynn took off his cap and held it over his heart for a moment of silence. There'd been no irony in his words, even though Louis knew that the sergeant shared their opinions about the foolishness of the orders that had led to the suicidal charge the day before.

"So," Flynn said, "to reward us for all our sacrificin', the army will not be replacing him. Instead, our own dear brigade is itself to be consolidated into the Third Brigade of the Second

Division under the command of Colonel Thomas Carroll. 'Tis an ungracious and ungenerous measure, but it's not for us to decide. The Irish Brigade as it once was is no more, though the name will still be used for our command unit."

Flynn's face looked so dark and dismal that Louis wished he could think of some words to say to encourage him. Seeing their sturdy sergeant so cast down lowered their weary spirits even more.

Louis began to count them up in his head.

The Wilderness.

The Bloody Angle where Possum had died.

Then Scarecrow and Happy right after.

That awful fight where Captain Blake had fallen at his feet.

They'd lost Merry then too. But in a way that brought no hurt to his heart. The little private was safe at home. Louis had read aloud the letter Mary sent to him and the other men in their mess. She missed them and thought them—next to her husband—to be the finest men on all of God's green earth. She would always regard them as brothers. Her husband, though he'd walk with a cane all his life, had survived in good enough shape. She was nursing him back to health. The door to the O'Shea home would always be open for any and all of them. She'd always keep an extra place set at their table. Even Kirk had grown misty-eyed.

Then, after Mary left them, had come the crossing of the river.

Cold Harbor.

Petersburg. Those Maine innocents marching to their deaths.

Louis looked down at his boots. *And who'll be next?*

"Excuse me, sir," a voice said.

It was Devlin breaking the silence as usual—though with a question and not a song.

"I heard a rumor that we've a colonel or two forwarding the draft back in New York," Devlin said. "Won't that swell our ranks back up again?"

Flynn laughed, but the laugh was a bitter one. "And who do ye think they'll find to send us?" he said. "The best and the bravest have all volunteered by now and far too many of them are but faces beneath the sod. We'll be sent a batch of laggards and left-behinds who've finally joined up for nothing but the bounty."

Louis looked over at Bull Belaney, who raised an eyebrow back at him.

"Not all of us who signed for the money have turned out that bad," Louis said, surprising himself and Flynn.

Flynn took off his cap and dusted it with his meaty hand.

"Begorrah," he said in a softer voice as he looked around all that remained of his company, "I'm not meanin' t' speak ill of any man here. Ye've been fine lads, every one of ye. I know that among ye are men who signed for the bounty and turned out to be tigers. What worries me now is that the ones they'll be getting through their draft—forced to join up whether they like it or no—will be as green as the grass and just as witless. And when the first shots are fired, where do ye suppose they'll go?"

CHAPTER TWENTY-EIGHT
THE MINE

Thursday, July 28, 1864

Louis stood ramrod straight as he handed the thick sheaf of papers to the officer.

Courier duty. A sight better to carry paper than a rifle and a pack. Even if the papers end up weighing more.

Observing how the rough plank table was piled high with white pages, he had to hold back a smile.

You could build a barricade five feet high around this camp with all the paper used every week by this Grand Army of the Potomac.

At least three copies of every order and everything else under the sun put down on paper.

Muster sheets listing how many men were in each company and regiment.

Requisition sheets for anything from blankets to ammunition.

Quartermaster reports, making careful note of everything in the way of supplies that went in and out, not counting what was stolen or sold on the side.

Maneuver orders—more hopeful guesses than accurate predictions.

General reports—what the officers said happened, as opposed to what really took place.

Promotions and reassignments—some political, some deserved, some too late for men already reassigned to the grave.

And thinking of paper . . .

Louis felt his pocket. The latest letter from his mother was still there.

> The money you ask about in your letter,
> that promised for your signing it was paid.
> That big-toothed lawyer, he took some. But
> still, even after the land payment, I have
> more than one hundred dollars. I have also
> gotten the paper for the sixteen dollars you
> have sent me for your first month's pay.
> I now tell you more, my son, about our
> piece of land up on the mountain above the
> town. I have found much of the good medicine
> plants, muskrat root and ginseng and all

others for healing. Ash trees, black ash, they are plenty for our making of baskets. Also the maples are good and big for sugar and higher up is the pine and cedar and spruce. There is a fine view, all the way to Vermont. In the pond close by we catch pickerel and perch. I know how much you love not just the catching of the fish, but the way I fry them for you in the skillet over the open fire. Azonis, she is the one who catches fish with me, she I have taught how to cook the fish as I do.

I do well. Last week I help five babies to be born. Also one man with fever and another with snake bite I make get well.

There will be much for you to do when you come home soon, my son. Good work in the town. They have build a race track for the running of the horses. John Morrissey, the one who was the fighter, he is the one who makes it, this horse track. It will bring more people to buy our baskets.

Azonis, she says these next words.

Louis, I think of you. You come home soon.
Your Mother,
Sophie

Come home soon.

He would write his mother—and, yes, Azonis—later that day. He would tell them that he was healthy and whole. But he would not say anything about being home soon.

This war is going to last a while. Unless maybe the mine works.

He took out a kerchief and stopped to wipe his forehead. All around him people were either moving about listlessly or seeking the shade. The only spot where hard work went on without cease was in the little valley below the abandoned railroad cut. That was where Louis was headed.

Louis squeezed some of the moisture out of his kerchief and watched as the drops of sweat were quickly absorbed into the dry red dirt. Hot as June had been, July was hotter. If Old Jeff Davis was the devil, as his friend Jeff said, then the head of the Rebels had to be pleased as all get out about this summer. All you needed was the smell of brimstone to think you were in that fiery place where Père Andre said the unrepentant sinners ended up. Even at midnight, heat still rose up from the Southern soil. Hot as blazes.

It wasn't just this heat that might make the Rebel president and his generals grin like demons. The months just past had been one disaster after another for the Union. Louis wiped his head again with the kerchief and made his way around a line of unhitched wagons. Some of the men from the Ninth were behind the wagons, laughing and joking as they played cards.

Louis raised his hand in a friendly wave.

They smiled and waved back. None of them seemed to be sweating.

Why is it that those fellows aren't bothered so much by the heat? Is it because their ancestors came from Africa? Or is it just that they were born down here?

"Louis," one of the men yelled, "y'all wanta play?"

"Maybe later," Louis called back.

Since Jeff had introduced Louis to some of his friends in the Ninth Corps, those men knew Louis by sight and always said howdy. Jeff's own Eighteenth Corps wasn't part of the big plan, but the black men of the Ninth were mightily involved.

The Ninth had been drilling, practicing maneuvers they'd soon be called upon to undertake. Pour through the breach blasted in the Rebel lines to take the rail hub of Petersburg in one quick thrust.

Providing the thing works.

Louis had his doubts that the explosion would do more than shake the earth under the Southerners' feet.

One of the colored soldiers farther back from the card players made eye contact with Louis. He nodded at the skillet he held over a fire and then touched his lips.

Eat with me?

Gabriel, one of Jeff's cousins. They'd belonged to the same white master and worked together building this section of the Dimmock Line. Gabriel's skin was a lighter brown than Louis's. He was slightly built and short and looked younger than Louis's own fifteen years. Louis had asked him how old he was. But Gabriel's answer had been the one many black soldiers gave to such a question.

"My ole massah didn't keep record of such things. Ole nuff t' work is all."

Louis held up his right hand, palm out, pointed with his chin in the direction he was going, then nodded back toward Gabriel.

Got somewhere to go, maybe later?

Gabriel's answering smile and nod showed he understood. Like Indians, former slaves knew how to get things across to each other without using words.

Louis started down the slope to the hole in the bank out of sight of the Southern fortifications 150 yards uphill. Different today down near the mouth of the mine. Before there'd been two long lines of men at work. One line lugging away buckets of earth or pushing wheelbarrows cobbled together from hardtack boxes. The other line bringing in timbers and planks salvaged from an abandoned sawmill to use for shoring.

Today, though, there was only one line. Nervous-looking men unloading and carrying in kegs of black powder.

Oh my!

Louis sat down under the thin shade of a small scrub pine to watch.

The rail-thin sergeant standing down by the wagons and supervising had explained the operation to Louis. His name was Harry Reese. Like others of the 48th Pennsylvania he'd been a hard coal miner before the war. Like so many other sergeants in the Union Army, he was a friend of Flynn's. That was how Louis had come to meet Reese three weeks ago near the start of July, when things had settled in to a blessedly quiet stand-off between the two armies.

"Louis, m'lad," Sergeant Flynn had said, "come t' me here. I've a wee errand for ye. Run this pouch of tobaccy over t' me friend Sergeant Reese in the Forty-eighth. Take yer time. With that inquirin' mind of yers, ye might find it interestin' to see what those boys are up to."

Interesting *hardly describes it.*

The idea had come from the 48th's regimental commander, Lieutenant Colonel Henry Pleasants. Have his mining lads drive a shaft under the enemy fort up the hill, pack it with powder, and blow a hole in the enemy line.

The higher-ups had scoffed at first. A tunnel of that length was impossible without air vents, vents that would give them away to the enemy. The earth would cave in on them. Even if they could do it, the enemy would hear their digging and countermine. Plus, it would take months.

But Pleasants, who'd been a civil engineer, drew up a sketch that caught the fancy of the commander of the Ninth Corps, Major General Ambrose Burnside. Burnside took it to General Meade. Meade's approval was halfhearted. He never expected it to succeed. But it would be a diversion for men getting bored after days of inaction.

"The great and good General Meade, he did not give us even a shovel, y' know," Sergeant Reese said as he stuffed his pipe with some of the tobacco Louis brought him. "Not a jot or a whittle did he have to spare for us. So we made do with what we had. Our blacksmiths fashioned picks from scrap metal and we made a pipe from wood to bring air in and another to draw it out by means of a fire we kept burning here on the outside. An old trick learnt from our Welsh grandfathers, y' know."

The sergeant nodded as he drew in on his pipe and then let out a contented breath of smoke. "Fine tobacco this, y' know."

That had been two weeks ago. Now, with those powder kegs being taken in, it looked as if the last stage of the plan was being put into motion.

Sergeant Reese beckoned to him. Louis got up and went down the hill.

"It's done?" Louis asked, handing the sergeant another pouch of Flynn's tobacco.

"Aye," Reese said, packing his pipe. "Our hard-working men, happy to dig in earth less unyielding than our hard stone of Pennsylvania, y'know, have done fine work. Look you. There before you is a five-hundred-and-eleven-foot shaft. Five feet high, four feet wide at the bottom and two feet wide at the top, all the way under the Rebel lines. This mornin' we finished the two lateral tunnels at the end to make a chamber beneath the enemy bastion."

"Right under the enemy fort?"

Reese nodded. "I was just in there an hour ago, y'know. And even through twenty feet of earth, I could still hear the thumping of Rebel soldiers walking above me."

"And the Rebel tunnels?"

Though the Pennsylvanians had kept as strict a silence as possible during the tunneling, the Southerners seemed to have caught on that a tunnel was being dug. Two weeks ago the Union miners had heard the first sounds of digging from the other side—two countermines being driven toward them.

Reese chuckled. "Through the grace of God or bad engineering, their tunnels missed us clean, y'know. And there's been no sound of their excavatin' for three days now. Let's move a ways up the hill, lad. We'd not be wanting a spark near those ammo wagons, y' know."

Fifty feet from the tunnel mouth and the nearest black powder keg, Reese pulled out a lucifer and struck it on the sole of his boot.

Reese puffed on his pipe. "Fine tobacco, this," he said again.

Louis looked back toward the dark mouth of the tunnel, imagining the closeness of that chamber where tons of explosive powder were being stacked.

All that powder, they're for sure going to blow something to Kingdom Come—most likely themselves!

"Y' want to go in and take a look, Chief?" Reese said, a wry smile on his face.

He already knows my answer. No way under heaven am I ever going into that tunnel.

He shook his head.

Reese nodded.

"Late for the Fourth of July, but we'll be having some fine fireworks soon, y' know."

CHAPTER TWENTY-NINE
THE FEINT

Saturday, July 30, 1864

Louis looked up from his whittling to cast an eye around the mid-afternoon camp. He was up on a little hill with his back against a tree. Below he could see the hundreds of tents in their regimental rows, like neat herds of white sheep. On the hillside next to him, Artis was stretched out with his cap over his eyes.

Not really sleeping, though.

Now that he and Artis were spending even more time together, he'd come to realize that his Mohawk friend hardly ever slept. He'd catnap now and then, but if Louis should wake at three in the morning and look out of the tent, like as not there Artis would be stirring the fire with a stick.

The old warrior way that Papa told me about. That is what Artis follows. A man on the path of war sleeps light or not at all.

The consolidation of units had resulted in Artis and four other men from his old company being reassigned to E. None of them, though, had been Artis's friend, the good-natured bantering Irish soldier.

Louis had asked about O'Grady when Artis arrived.

Artis just shook his head and swung his hand palm downward. Louis understood. Don't say the names of the dead.

An already familiar face, Artis fit in easily as E Company settled into a routine like that of the men in all the other regiments dug in around Petersburg—Rebel and Yankee alike.

Drilling, eating, playing cards, and swapping stories and songs to ease the boredom. So the hot summer days passed. Sometimes they'd get up a game of baseball. Louis had never heard of it before joining the army. But soldiers like Bull, who came from New York City, were crazy for it.

Just yesterday baseball had been the source of a heated argument between Bull and Joker.

"Why, in Brooklyn alone," Belaney said with great fervor, "there's no fewer than three fine teams—the Stars, the Eckfords, and the Atlantics. And you should see what Candy Cummings of the Stars can do! He can hurl a ball in such a way that it scoots to the right or the left in flight."

"A curveball? Hah!" Kirk sniffed. "It's a myth. A scientific impossibility."

"I seed it with me own eyes."

"An optical illusion," Kirk replied. "Or maybe you had so many beers that it blurred your vision."

Belaney got so worked up about it that he'd insisted on the two of them taking a ball and going out to a level piece of ground. There Bull had tried for a solid hour without success to make a ball curve sideways through the air the way he swore his man Cummings could.

Today, though, was too torrid for even a game of pitch and catch. The few clouds in the sky were stuck in place, seemingly as stunned by the heat as the humans moving like tiny ants in the lines of trenches below.

Even the sharpshooters had been affected by the counterfeit peace between the two great armies. Almost no shots were being fired. In the twilight, informal truces sprang up between companies of young men in blue and gray.

At first, jests were traded back and forth across the no-man's-land between the Army of the Potomac and Lee's Army of Northern Virginia.

"Hey Yank, y'all still as good at runnin' as you was at Manassas?"

"Reb, any of you got any shoes left or has you et them all by now?"

Then, as the mid-summer quiet continued, a few from the two armies began to venture forth to meet in the middle and trade Southern tobacco—the only staple the ragged men in gray ever seemed to have in abundance—for sweets, a little salt pork, or even a few precious sheets of writing paper so that some homesick Carolinian might write a letter to his sweetheart or his mother.

But in that one little valley, despite the heat, feverish activity had been taking place as Pennsylvania miners, faces streaked with red clay and sweat, labored on their tunnel.

"We'll be filling in the tunnel for about forty feet, you know," Sergeant Reese had explained. "Tamped in tight like a stopper. The only thing that worries us now is whether or not we'll actually get it to blow when the time comes. Our request for insulated wire and a galvanic battery failed t' come through, y'know. So what we have is two fifty-foot fuses spliced together."

Quiet, but it's the calm before the thunder.

Sure enough, after the evening meal, things began to happen.

"It's a night march for us, men," Sergeant Flynn said. "And this time, saints be praised, it's along a well-marked road and we'll not get lost."

Before night fell, Second Corps was on the move. They struck out to the north, making no effort to hide their movements from the enemy.

Draw their attention away from the line that's to be blown up. With all this marching they're making us do, I just hope it makes something bigger than a woodchuck hole!

Their march was a long one, all the way up through the small peninsula to the spot on the curving James River where Tenth Corps had thrown a pontoon bridge across. The dawn was breaking as they made their attack on the works at Deep Bottom, the combined Irish Brigade at the front.

After three weeks of rest, Louis and the other men around him had thrown off the feeling of doom that oppressed them a month ago. The green regimental flag with its Irish harp waved proudly over their heads as they advanced into battle with a great shout.

They took the enemy so much by surprise that the fight was over almost before it started. In what seemed like the space of only a few heartbeats to Louis they found themselves in control of the first line of earthworks, four twenty-pounder Parrott guns, and two hundred Rebel prisoners. But there they stopped.

Their movement had been supposed to be little more than a feint to draw a large force up from the Petersburg line. Scouts reported that a large force of Rebel soldiers was being shifted their way to face what the Southern commanders feared was a major attempt to break through to Richmond.

Sergeant Flynn grinned as he passed on the orders to withdraw. "Sure and we've finally done something just as we'd planned," he said. Even Corporal Hayes had the hint of a smile on his face as they began their withdrawal to a stronger position.

Louis was assigned with his friends to guard one group of prisoners. As they marched along, some of the men in gray seemed eager to strike up friendly conversations. Most of them seemed relieved to have been captured and taken out of the fight. Also, orders had been given to feed the prisoners, who all were glad to have some food to put into their bellies.

"The way you Southern boys is chewing on hardtack," Joker said, "you'd think it was maple sugar."

"Never shoulda jined the infantry," replied a thin, long-haired Southern soldier. The skinny Rebel's clothes fit him like a scarecrow and his shoes were so worn out that the soles flapped against the ground as he walked. His voice, though, was pleasant and friendly. Everyone within earshot was finding the man's company amusing.

"Life in the infantry ain't worth a goober," the skinny Rebel explained. "Them cavalry boys has it good. Jest riding about and havin' a fine time. They never wants for food either. Jest grab up a chicken or a porker as they rides along an' then gallop away without a howdy-do and leave us to do the fightin'. No suh, if'n you wants to eat and can't arrange to be in the quartermaster's department or the commissary, then the cavalry is sure the place to be. And if it wasn't for the fact that ah just hates them stuck-up cavalrymen, ah would of been one of them. If'n ah could ride a horse, that is."

The man paused to lick the last crumbs of his piece of hardtack from his fingers, pushed the hair back from his eyes, and squinted over at Louis and Artis.

"You two Yanks colored boys?" he asked.

The man's tone wasn't unfriendly.

"Nope," Louis replied.

"Indian," Artis said.

"Unh-hunh, so you are. Wouldn't of mattered, though, if'n you was colored. Ah ain't got nothin' agin' the coloreds. Biggest mistake we ever made was not jest setting them all free onct the war began. Most of us fighting this war, they's poor folk like me. Never ownt a slave, never wanted one. We jest fightin' for our rahts since you Yankees invaded us. Them no-account senators we got up in Richmond, Lord, some of them got plantations with hundreds of darkies. They got more slaves than they got sense, if'n you know what ah mean."

Songbird had drifted closer as the man delivered his monologue.

"What do you mean by that?" Songbird asked.

"Wull," the talkative Rebel said, "jest that aside from Jeff Davis, who appears to have a head on his shoulders, about all them men supposed to be representin' us does is argue with each other like mules. Now, ah was a farmer afore all this begun. Worked twenty acres with my ma and my pa and my two brothers. And one thing ever' soul who works the soil knows is that if'n you got a crop, you needs to sell it if'n you wants the money to live on. That's jest one thing them mules in fine suits up in Richmond is too dumb to figger out."

"What's your meaning?" Devlin said.

"Cotton," the man said. There was a different look about him now. Although the ragged young Southerner had seemed at first like a country bumpkin, Louis saw the intelligence in the man's eyes.

"Cotton?"

"Cotton, the sale of which would've paid for uniforms—not like these rags we're wearing—and food for us to eat. We grows the finest cotton in the world here in the South and the English would have kept on buying it from us, even if they was against slavery—which as ah said we should of just got rid of all on our own at the start of this set-to. So what did those eddicated idjits in Richmond do? They told the British they wouldn't sell any of our cotton to them unless they declared for our side against the North. But as long as we still got slaves, them English was not about to do that. So where's all our Southern cotton? Rottin' in warehouses for the last three years and not bringing in a dime."

Soon they reached the James River and crossed. Another company was waiting there to take the captives on to City Point. From there the Rebs would be sent north by ship to a POW camp.

Off to Elmira. And it's sad I am to think of you going there.

"Good luck to you, even if you is Yanks," the long-haired young Southerner shouted over his shoulder. He waved good-bye with his left hand since his right was clutching the additional pieces of hardtack that the men of E Company had given him.

"You too, Reb," Louis called back.

It was another long march through the dark from Deep Bottom back to Petersburg. A beautiful dawn began to break over the hills. The sky streaked with rose red and burnished gold. Small birds fluttered up in the air to twitter their songs to welcome the new day, seemingly unaware of the war going on between the two-leggeds camped in the woods and fields and crouched in the trenches around them.

Louis took a deep breath of the sweet morning air. He turned toward Artis and opened his mouth. But whatever words he had planned to say were never spoken. There was a sudden deep crumping sound. The two of them felt as much as heard it. The earth under their feet shuddered like a beaten horse.

Louis squinted his eyes toward the part of the line a mile ahead where the Pennsylvania miners had been laboring for the past month.

Where . . . ?

Just time enough to think that word before the answer was made brutally clear.

A great column of smoke and earth shot up, sudden as a giant's fist thrust into the air. Even as far away as they were, the massive cloud lifted up and up above them. It was so huge that Louis immediately felt the wrongness of it. It shot out sparks of fire, and flashes of lightning as it rose, formless at first, then taking the shape of a dark arching elm with a trunk made of fire. Two heartbeats later a sound like the roaring of a huge hungry beast struck them, so loud it was deafening.

Men around Louis and Artis shrank back from what seemed like the end of the world. Some covered their faces or dropped to the ground. But the two young Indian soldiers did not look away. Their keen eyes saw what was falling out of that cloud. Earth, broken timbers, stones—and what looked to be blackened human limbs.

"Good God!" Artis said.

Louis shook his head. "Nothing good about this."

A thunder crash of cannons came hard on the heels of the blast. One hundred and forty-four field pieces had been lined up for the assault to follow the setting off of the mine. It seemed as if every mortar and siege gun let go at once as shocked artillery men pulled their lanyards. But there was no second round, no answering fire. A brittle silence hung over the lines. Both sides were stunned by the largest explosion ever set off by human hands.

"What have we gone and done?" Louis said as the men of his company slowly rose to their feet around him and Artis. "What have we gone and done?"

CHAPTER THIRTY
THE CRATER

Monday, August 8, 1864

Louis and Artis kept low as they made their way over to the new camp of the 48th. In the week since the explosion the Pennsylvanians had been moved farther back from the great hole that had once been a section of the Rebel line. The Confederate sharpshooters over there were all as angry as hornets now. Any Union soldier who raised his head was in danger of losing it.

No more informal truces now between us and the boys in gray.

Just as he thought that, he heard the sudden whish of air.

Both Louis and Artis flinched, even though it was already too late to duck.

Crack! A minié ball buried itself in the log abutment a hand's breadth above their heads. Some sniper in gray must have climbed to a treetop high enough to get a line of sight over the top of the fortification. The two boys duckwalked the rest of the way along the ditch, then cut downhill.

"Thank ye both," Sergeant Reese said as he accepted the small packet of tobacco that Sergeant Flynn had sent over.

The three of them sat under a wide-trunked Southern oak behind the camp of the 48th. From the leafy branches above them small birds in a hidden nest cheeped, uninterested in the doings of the humans below.

No wars for them. There's times I'd like to be a bird.

Reese's voice cut into his reverie. "Now, you and your friend would be wanting to hear more of the story, won't you?"

"Please, sir," Artis said. Artis might joke with his friends, but he was always unfailingly polite to anyone older than himself.

Louis nodded agreement.

This was the real reason they'd been sent on this errand—to bring back Reese's side of the story to Flynn. A thousand tales were being told in camp of all that occurred on that dreadful day. Yet awful as the events had been, everyone wanted to hear more—as if hearing it might make another great failure easier to bear. To hear the most, you had to go to those who always know the most—the sergeants.

"The grand foolishness began the night before," Reese said, packing his pipe and lighting it. "And the higher they go, the bigger the fools they are, y' know. General Burnside was happily goin' about his business, all his plans neatly laid for the morrow, when what should come to him but a courier from army headquarters. 'Twas a message from our grand generals Meade and Grant. Instead of having the assault led by the Colored Troops of the Ninth who'd been rehearsing the plan for days, the attack was now to be spearheaded by one of the white divisions."

"Oh my!" Artis said, raising an eyebrow.

"And well might ye say that," Reese agreed. He reached down, picked something up, held it before his eyes, and studied it.

A wood splinter. Even here, half a mile away, bits of debris fell from that godawful blast.

Reese used the splinter to tamp down the tobacco in his pipe. "And why would the high and mighty of the army be changing the plan at the last moment, y' might ask? Well, this is an election year, y'know. And there's been one embarrassment after another for our generals and our president. The Bloody Angle, Cold Harbor, and then this month past there was that hell-be-damned raid of Jubal Early's."

Louis nodded his head.

He'd read about the daring Southern general's exploit in a three-week-old *New York Herald* Bull bought from a sutler. To the shock of the entire Union, General Early had led a hand-picked force of 10,000 Confederate veterans north. With so many federal troops massed around Petersburg, he marched through Maryland with little opposition and crossed the Potomac on July 5.

Early's small army came within a mile of capturing Washington. The city militia, the office personnel, and the war invalids were all brought to its defense. The veterans' hospitals emptied of anyone who could limp to the lines. President Lincoln refused to go into hiding, even though he'd been warned about secessionist plots to assassinate him. Instead, he traveled on horseback from one end of Washington to another during the siege. Lincoln even came under fire himself as he stood on the parapet of Fort Stevens, an inviting target for the Rebel marksmen a thousand yards away. Minié balls began whizzing past the lanky man in black whose unusual height and tall stovepipe hat made him tower two feet above everyone else. When an officer standing next to the president was struck by one of those sniper rounds, someone yelled, "Get down, you damn fool, before you get shot!" not knowing he was directing his remarks at the leader of the Union. An amused smile on his face, the Great Emancipator had finally climbed down.

The arrival of reinforcements had forced General Early to grudgingly withdraw on the twelfth of July. But as he moved back down through Pennsylvania he collected huge sums of gold and greenbacks from the cities he passed by threatening to burn them to the ground if they refused to pay up. The blackened ruins of Chambersburg attested to the seriousness of his threats.

"So," Sergeant Reese continued, "if Honest Abe hoped to hang on to his high office and not lose to some 'Peace-at-all-costs Democrat' like McClellan, 'twould not have been good for him to have yet another great embarrassment. Such as having his generals shove a corps of poor untested Negroes into battle to be slaughtered. Thus, in their great wisdom, Meade and Grant decided we had to show how much we cared for our Colored Troops by doing the one thing that would get them killed. Hold them back till things got so desperate they had to let them go. Ah, and they got desperate fast enough, y' know."

The sergeant puffed again at his pipe.

Louis and Artis waited.

"Now they had to choose which unrehearsed white division would be the lucky one to take the forefront. No one volunteered, so Burnside had his three commanders draw straws. As evil luck would have it, the one who got the short straw was the worst of them all."

Reese spat onto the ground. "Brigadier General James H. Ledlie. There's a man fierce at fighting—a bottle. And where was he during the whole sorry affair? As soon as that explosion went off, he scuttled down to the bombproof with a quart of rum. There he stayed for the whole day, you know. Not only that, General Ferraro, the man supposed to be commanding the Colored Troops, he joined him."

Reese puffed out a ring of smoke, then shifted to cross his legs. "The fuse was lit at three a.m. Half an hour passed and it still hadn't gone. So we knew it must have burned out at the splice, just as we'd feared. So it was back into the tunnel for Lieutenant Douty and me. Cut the fuse, relight it, and run like rabbits being chased by a weasel! It went up just as we got out. I was deaf for a whole day after, y' know. Ach! The hole it made! Sixty feet wide and a hundred feet long! Thirty feet deep with sides of steep clay. Have y' seen it?"

"No," Louis said.

"Not likely we'd be here if we had," Artis added.

Sergeant Reese nodded. "Of course not. Try to take a peek now, y'll get your head taken off by some Southern sniper. The Johnnies are a wee bit peeved with us for blowing up their fort, y' know. And along with that fine fort and all its guns, three hundred Rebels or more was blown sky-high as well."

Reese puffed out another ring of smoke and watched as it dissipated slowly in the still air around them.

"Now, blowing all that up was according to plan. 'Twas just, y' might say, a mite too successful. Everyone was so scared by the great force of it that they ran in the other direction. Not just the graybacks, but our men in blue as well. It took the officers half an hour to get 'em turned around and headed back. And where do y' think they marched?"

"Into the crater," Artis said.

"Aye. It seems that in the confusion, our side forgot a wee part of the grand plan, which was to move the barricades to either side of the hole. So what did those advancing men see before them? Naught but a ten-foot-wide passway straight down into the crater. Now don't forget that the only ones who'd been rehearsed was those Colored Troops who'd been sent away to the rear. So where else could those soldiers in Ledlie's division go without their leader to tell them but down into that bloody hole, y' know? Leaping in as if it was the world's biggest trench where they might be safe from the enemy's guns."

Reese cleared his throat and spat. "Once in, of course, with not a ladder among them and those clay sides so slippery and crumbling, they were caught like fish in a barrel. The second division and the third followed right behind, swarming down into that crater for cover. Then the colored boys arrived."

Sergeant Reese looked off to the place where the survivors of General Ferraro's troops had their camp.

"Those Negro lads was singing," Reese said, tapping his chin with his pipe. "Now how did that song go?"

"We looks like men a-marchin' on, we looks like men of war?" Louis ventured.

Gabriel and the men in the camp of the Ninth had been singing it the week before.

"Indeed," Reese said, tapping the air with his pipe. "The very song. And they did look like men of war—or at least men with some brains in their heads. Instead of going into that crater, they swung to either side to take the heights. With any support they might have made it, y' know. But those Rebels had recovered and were pouring back to their wrecked line. Those brave black lads ended up being driven back into that infernal hole with all the other unfortunate souls."

Heat rose from the quiet field behind them. Even the small birds in the tree above them had grown quiet.

Louis thought about all the men lost in the Battle of the Crater. He'd heard the figures from Flynn. Thirteen hundred men from the Ninth, Gabriel among them. Twice that many in the white divisions. Bad as Cold Harbor, maybe worse.

Artis cleared his throat.

"God save us from all generals," he said.

Sergeant Reese spat again. "Amen to that."

CHAPTER THIRTY-ONE
CITY POINT

Saturday, August 13, 1864

Moles. That's what we've become.

In the bitter weeks following the Battle of the Crater, the tents and huts near the line were no longer safe. Every day men were being struck by snipers' rounds piercing the thin walls of canvas or brush.

It was fall back or make better fortifications. So the whole Union Army moved more or less underground, down into deep trenches as heavily reinforced as bombproof forts. A soldier might now spend a whole day without the light of the sun touching his face.

Here and there, the rough humor of men at war showed

itself in hand-lettered signs placed by the entrances of those man-made caves.

Louis read the newest one nailed to the timbers of the bombproof he passed on his way to morning drill.

HOTEL COMFORT
REASONABLE RATES

The man just inside the door waved as he passed. The face wasn't familiar, but Louis waved back. More and more folks seemed to recognize him now—the big Indian from the Irish Brigade

"Hey Chief," the man yelled, "you hear how the Rebs blowed up City Point?"

Louis nodded and continued on.

Old news by now. Four whole days ago. Plus we all heard the danged thing go up. Like it was right next door and not eight miles away.

City Point. Grant's headquarters. Placed on the peninsula where the Appomattox River joined the James, it was the nerve center and supply depot for the operations of the Army of the Potomac in Virginia. What had been a sleepy little tobacco town was now one of the biggest ports in North America.

Louis thought about what it must have been like last Saturday, just at noon. Grant sitting in front of his tent looking out at the peaceful river where a supply barge full of artillery ammunition and supplies was sitting at anchor.

Wha-boom!

The whole barge had gone sky-high in a blast that rivaled the one two weeks earlier at the Crater. Forty-three men had been killed and hundreds injured, not just by the explosion but by the debris that rained down, including hundreds of new saddles intended for Sheridan's cavalry.

Awful as it was, Louis had to smile at the thought of those saddles flapping down out of the sky like giant bats.

They say one of them landed right at General Grant's feet.

But the shower of shot, shell, pieces of wood, iron bolts, and bars and pieces of chain that put holes in his tent had left the Union's commander uninjured.

Word was that it was sabotage. A Confederate agent had given a wooden box to a crew member, telling him it was from the captain and should be stowed down below with the cargo. It had been a bomb with a clockwork mechanism and some black powder in it.

It's like the story of this whole war. One little box doing as much for the Rebs in five minutes as a whole corps of men did for us in weeks of digging. And without a single enemy soldier lost, to boot.

When Louis reached the place where the Second Corps had been camped, what he saw surprised him. Everyone was packing.

The tent he shared with Artis had already been struck. Artis had rolled up Louis's blanket and laid out his gear to make it easier to pack.

"We're pulling out, Chief," Kirk said. "Our destination is a great mystery."

Devlin grinned. "Wherever we're going, short of the gates of Hell, it has to be better than here."

"Or so you hope," Belaney added.

As they started their march, Louis looked back over his shoulder at the arid, desolate, battle-scarred plain outside Petersburg.

Me, I am glad to leave this place behind.

Their line of march reached City Point at noon. There, when they bivouaced, a pleasant surprise appeared. Not just the usual coffee and hardtack, but fresh-baked bread from the bakery on the grounds.

"'Tis said they're baking a hundred thousand a day," Sergeant Flynn said, tearing off a piece from the warm loaf in his hand. "And look ye over there."

Was it possible?

"Apples and pears!" Artis said in stunned delight.

"And that's not the only sweet thing here," Belaney said. The reverence in his tone was like that usually reserved for prayer. "Look at those lasses!"

Louis had been so overwhelmed by the sheer size of City Point, the thousand new sights, that he hadn't noticed what else was truly different about this place. The presence of the fairer sex.

Mon Dieu, there's females everywhere.

It wasn't that he'd not been seeing women over the past four months. Women dressed like women, that is, and not disguised like a man as Mary had been. There'd always been some women around Petersburg or any of the places the Army of the Potomac pitched their tents for more than a night. Some were wives and daughters of sutlers, some were laundresses plying their trade. Others were daughters of Eve earning a living in a less respectable way.

Louis's face grew red as he thought about them. He had no experience with those fallen angels, but he'd heard other older soldiers speak of those women with their forward ways and extravagant clothes.

Fallen angels, Cyprians, ladies of the evening. Those were some of the names he'd heard them called.

These women here at City Point, though, didn't look like the ladies of the night. Their demeanor and dress were modest. They walked with purpose as if on their way to accomplish worthy tasks.

Louis tried not to stare.

"True angels of mercy," Flynn said in a surprisingly tender voice, putting a meaty hand on Louis's shoulder. "Nurses come t' care for our sick and injured. They make me think of me own sweet, modest Lizzy back home in Boston."

Louis turned to look at Flynn. Lizzy? He'd never thought of his sergeant as being anything but a soldier, not a man with someone waiting for him back home. Was that a tear in the corner of Flynn's eye?

Flynn patted Louis's shoulder once more and then turned to walk down the pier.

Louis looked again at the purposeful women around them.

Women nurses. I've read about them.

The Women's Nursing Corps. Another new thing brought into being by this war. Louis took note of the plain brown or black dresses that marked those women as nurses. Standard uniforms for those allowed to join the organization founded by a woman named Dorothea Dix early on in the war.

What was it I saw in the New York Herald *about them?*

"If a woman is too fond of adorning herself with finery or her face is pretty, she shall be judged unsuitable to join."

Modest and plain, that was how a nurse was supposed to be.

"Let's get us some of that fruit," Artis said.

"Huh?" Louis said. "Oh." His friend was pointing with his chin toward the commissary workers with the baskets of apples and pears.

Joker, Songbird, and Bull joined them. The five made their way over to the edge of the pier where the fruit had been unloaded. Fifty yards downriver from them were broken and blackened timbers—signs of the recent catastrophe.

"Guess you had some fun here last week," Kirk said to an old man with a thick gray beard handing out apples from a basket.

The old man jerked his head toward the right. "Y' wanta hear 'bout that," he said, "y'ought spen' some time with them fellas over there what seen it firsthand."

Louis and Joker looked in the direction the man indicated. A wide field spread with hundreds of tents stretched off into the distance.

"Depot Field Hospital," the old man said proudly. "Two hunnerd acres 'n' ten thousand beds. Makes it 'bout the biggest hospital in the world, don't it? A right popular place. Men's jest dying t' get in there." He guffawed at his own joke.

The five of them took their food to sit in the shade of a tree. As the breeze from the river washed over him, an unfamiliar feeling of contentment came to Louis.

I wouldn't mind spending some time here.

A shadow fell across his feet.

"Don't get too comfortable, men."

The five men looked up at Corporal Hayes, pointing up the river with a hand that held a half-eaten apple.

"Re-forming the company over there. Boarding that barge in ten minutes."

Louis looked up and his eyes met those of their corporal.

Here we go again, the look on Hayes's face said.

As soon as the last man had tromped across the planks, the transport barges began to steam away, heading east from City Point. Joker elbowed his way next to Louis, who stood leaning over the rail.

"A fine rumor's being spread," Kirk said, putting an arm around Louis's shoulders. "If we go downriver they'll be sending us to Washington so as we can help recruit and train more men to fill in the gaps. And wouldn't that be fine?"

"Better," Louis said. "Too good to be true."

Downriver. Out of the fighting?

At Wilson's Landing, twelve miles below the point, they anchored for the evening. At midnight, though, the anchors were weighed and the engines reversed. Back upriver they went until the light of dawn showed their true destination. They pulled in to shore by a familiar-looking pontoon bridge.

"Deep Bottom," Corporal Hayes said in a sepulchral tone.

We've been here before.

"Lads," Flynn intoned, his voice heavy with irony, "once again our orders are easy ones. Our simple task is t' break through the Rebel lines and take Richmond."

CHAPTER THIRTY-TWO
REAMS STATION

Wednesday, August 24, 1864

Louis sat back to back with Artis as they refilled their cap boxes from the new supply of shiny copper percussion caps, each shaped like a little top hat.

More than a week had passed since they'd disembarked from the transport barges and made their first two-hour march. Under the blazing sun of midday, it had been so hot that two men fell dead out of the line of march from heatstroke. And that had just been the start of their trial by fire.

A few yards away from them, Songbird was recounting the latest battle at Deep Bottom to an awed circle of recruits—brand-new arrivals about to be pressed into service for the first time in this campaign.

You can almost read the word green *on their foreheads. No need to learn their names. They won't last long enough.*

Meanwhile, Songbird's words were coming close to a martial hymn.

"New earthworks had been thrown up near the New Market Road since our previous battles. Impregnable, they seemed, perched high as hawks on the steep hill above us," Devlin intoned. "But the brave remnants of our brigade pushed forward, bent double from the effort, holding our fire, whilst ball and shell buzzed above us like great evil bees. Brigadier General Francis Barlow of the First Division—brave soldier but a petty man—had doubted from the start we could prevail. He was sure that we'd be broken, but we did not fail. With a great-throated shout that near drowned out even the roar of shot and shell, we rushed like a sweeping tempest through the foe. 'Twas a grand victory."

Louis fastened the cap box shut at the exact same moment as Artis.

The two exchanged a nod and a glance, then began filling their cartridge boxes with .58-caliber ammunition at the same rapid clip.

Victory. You might call it that if you don't count the cost.

Reinforcements had come up against them, their advance had been halted. Under a flag of truce the two sides had spent the better part of the next day retrieving and burying their dead.

Their job now was to move on Reams Station to destroy the Weldon railroad. Only lightly defended—or so they were told.

So few of us veterans left, it had better be that. New fish trying to swim against the tide? Draftees, not worth the powder to blow them to Kingdom Come.

Men forced into the army would as often run as fight. Not like the friends who'd been by his side and, by the grace of Ktsi Nwaskw, still remained there. Somehow, those closest to him since Merry's departure had survived. Devlin and Kirk, Belaney, Corporal Hayes, Sergeant Flynn and Artis. The six of them, himself making it a lucky seven. All there was of a platoon that had once numbered twenty in an Irish Regiment of a thousand that was now fewer than five hundred men.

What odds does that set against any of us getting through another fight? Our luck is due to run out. Overdue.

He finished filling the cartridge box, raised his hands, and looked over at Artis—who had finished a moment ahead of him and wore a small satisfied smile.

"That makes two apples you owe me," Artis drawled.

"If I ever see one again," Louis said.

They glanced over at one of the groups of new men sitting together fifty feet away from Artis and him. Confused farm boys who'd been forced into the army like cattle being driven to the stockyard. One of them, who was having a hard time fumbling his caps into the box, lifted his head to smile at them. Louis quickly turned away.

No. I don't want to make any more friends and see them get killed.

He turned his eyes toward the sky, listening for a rumble of thunder. Back home they'd be harvesting the green corn now. How long had it been since he'd had any thoughts in his mind of working the land rather than fighting to take it? It seemed forever. But in terms of days and weeks, in truth, not that long.

August 25th tomorrow. May 4th when we crossed the Rapidan. Three months and eleven days.

As planned, they moved out at dawn. Their position was to the left of the Fifth Corps. But as they began to tear up the rails, they were attacked from the flank and the rear. In no time at all, the twelve pieces of artillery they'd brought to the battle were taken by the Confederate soldiers and turned on them. No support from the new recruits. Once the fighting began, the entire division refused to move forward or discharge their weapons. The Irish Brigade was on its own.

Louis heard the sick thud of a minié ball striking flesh. He looked to his left. Belaney lay on the ground beside him, his face pale and blood pouring from a great wound in his shoulder.

Louis reached toward Bull. Someone grabbed at his coat. Sergeant Flynn.

"There," Flynn shouted, pushing him back, pointing to a line of partially dug trench near the station. Other members of the Brigade were already taking cover there.

"Behind them breastworks."

Sergeant Flynn's hat flew off. He clutched at his temple. He took two slow steps and toppled like a great oak tree.

Someone else pulling at Louis's arm. Artis.

Artis's lips moved. Louis couldn't hear the words. There was a roaring in his ears like a storm wind.

Move! Artis was mouthing. *Move.*

Louis willed his feet forward, found himself kneeling behind the wall of earth Flynn had pointed to before being hit.

Corporal Hayes was shouting orders, tears streaming down his face, dripping off the ends of his mustache.

Keep it up! Pour it on.

The charge came at them.

They fired and loaded, fired and loaded. The Rebels fell back.

Another charge. Fire and load. Fire and load. One wave of Rebel attackers after another.

Such desperate courage in those grayback boys who refused to quit.

Handle. Tear. Charge. Draw. Ram. Prime. Shoulder. Aim. Fire!

I wish there was some other way.

Another wave of enemy soldiers hit the entrenchment. Corporal Hayes grappled with a Southerner whose bearded face and dark-stained uniform made him look more like a bear than a man. They fell over the breastworks and were lost from Louis's sight.

More cannons firing on them. A Union officer with the insignia of a lieutenant shouting.

Abandon the works.

Crouching, moving back. Joker lurching as if struck in his side by a great hammer. No time to stop. Load and fire.

In the woods now. Trees giving some cover, not enough. A great splinter of wood flying from the pine next to him. A mist of red springing up from Songbird's neck, his finger pulling the trigger of his Springfield that fired one last time as he crumpled.

All of them but Artis and me.

He tried to raise his rifle to his shoulder. To his surprise there was no strength in his arms. Not only that, he was no longer standing. For some reason he was on his back. A warm wet feeling on his side. His left leg was splayed out at a strange angle. His blue trousers turning bright red at his lower thigh. Red. Crimson red, the color of a cardinal's wing spreading wider.

No pain. Hard to speak or breathe. No sounds of thunder. No sound at all.

The sky. There, up through gaps in the trees where exploding shells knocked out the tops of the forest. Clouds in the sky, white cotton on blue cloth.

Not dark yet.

"*Nigawes,*" he whispered.

Then his voice would no longer work. So, in his mind he called, called with all his heart.

Nigawes, my mother. Come help me!

Then it was dark. Very dark.

CHAPTER THIRTY-THREE
DEPOT HOSPITAL

Why am I stuck in this fog?

The deep darkness was receding. But it was not being banished by daylight. A grayness thick as cotton circled his aching head. Blurry shapes came and went each time he managed to briefly open his eyes. The voices he heard were distant—like those from boats passing on an unseen river, coming close, drifting away again.

"No, wait. These two are alive . . ."

"Can't get him to let go of his rifle . . ."

". . . almost there now, just . . ."

Those words almost made sense. Hard to pay attention to them, though. Feeling in his arms and legs was returning.

With it a pain so bone deep, it made him clench his teeth and moan.

"... you're hurting him, be ..."

He tried to make sense of those broken pieces of sight and sound. Making sense helped him get hold of the pain and push it down.

I'm alive.

That made sense. Everything shaking around him. Sounds he knew. Clopping. Rattling. A horse's hooves. A wagon.

I'm on a battlefield ambulance.

Black seeped back, ink tipped from a bottle. Heavy black, threatening to drown him in endless dark.

Wait. There's a light.

A wigwam. A fire burning inside. He was kneeling by the door, looking in, recognizing the man on the other side of the fire.

"*Mitongwes,*" Louis said, "my father."

His vision was blurred, but he saw the glad smile on his father's face. Louis could crawl in from the darkness and pain and be with him.

Jean Nolette held up his hand, palm out.

"*Nda,*" he said, his voice strong. "Not yet, my son."

Louis opened his eyes. A face not his father's was so close that he could smell the man's whiskey breath.

"Still with us, soldier? Good. I'm a doctor. You're in Second Corps Hospital at City Point."

Someone tugging at his clothes, a ripping sound. He tried to sit up, lifted his shoulders off the cot.

"Hold him down!" the doctor yelled.

Dark again. Not as much as before. As if he were in a room where everything connected to light and life was on the other side of a thin wall.

Someone was screaming.

"Don't cut off my leg. Don't cut off my leg."

Then a terrible sound like wood being sawed—except it wasn't wood.

Another voice.

"Tie it off tighter. Stop the blood."

Louis recognized that voice. The doctor who'd just been talking to him.

Whose voice was screaming? Mine?

Quieter. Darker. No thinking or dreaming.

The next time Louis knew he was awake. Knew where he was. On a cot in Depot Hospital. He looked up at the ceiling of the big tent. He remembered it all. The battle, his friends falling, the shell that burst overhead, the darkness that came and went, the dream of his father that was more than a dream.

The bone saw and that voice screaming.

His leg ached. He didn't dare look down.

"Hey, Chief."

Louis weakly turned his head to the right. A man whose worn face was familiar, though it looked twenty years older, was smiling weakly at him.

"Bull," Louis whispered

"Yup," Belaney replied. "'Tis me, or what's left of me." He gestured down. Bull Belaney's left leg was gone below the knee.

Louis raised his head. It took much of his strength and hurt like blue blazes, but he had to see. He let out the breath he had been holding.

Merci, mon Dieu.

His own two legs were there, wrapped in bandages, but entire.

"That ether is something," Bull said. "'Tis like floating up on a cloud into heaven. The nurse said I was bellowing like a bull when they took it off, but I dunna remember a blessed thing."

"I'm sorry," Louis rasped.

Bull shook his head. "It's all right, bucko. The war is done for me. I'll have me pension and that'll be money enough to bring me sainted mother over to live with me. I'll get me one of them cork legs and dance a jig afore the year's out."

Louis looked at the man who'd seemed mean and selfish, but proved true as any man in their company. He managed to reach his hand over to grasp Belaney's.

"Proud to have served with you, Bull."

Belaney grinned. "For you to make a speech as long as that, Chief, you must be proud indeed. The doctor told me you have more holes in you than a leaky rowboat."

"Just you and me?" Louis asked. Had others of their small company survived?

"Now there's a tale t' tell," Belaney said. Was he smiling? "We . . ."

Bull's voice was getting fainter. His mouth was moving. No words seemed to be coming out of it. The bright light of day that had been streaming in through the tent a moment ago was failing.

When he opened his eyes again, a man in a blood-spattered tunic was bending over his leg. The bandages had been removed, cut free by the scalpel the man held in his left hand. The man probed a dirty finger into the great gash in his left thigh.

"Feel that, do you?" The doctor pressed harder. "Pain?"

Louis gritted his teeth and nodded.

"Excellent," the doctor said, his voice brisk. "Your other wounds are inconsequential next to this one. Deep to the bone. But no arteries cut. Not as much blood lost as some. Now we must hope for the appearance of laudable pus." He straightened up and wiped his hands on his soiled shirt. "Nurse, new dressings on this one. Remember to keep them moist." The doctor's face blurred. A woman dressed in brown floated toward Louis, indistinct as a figure at the edge of a dream.

He wasn't sure how long he slept this time, but when he woke he was weak as a day-old pup. Belaney was no longer in the cot next to him. No one he knew anywhere in sight, though there were hundreds of men all around him—not just in this tent but in others he could see through the open flap. What had he been told about Depot Hospital?

Two hundred acres. Beds for ten thousand men.

He tried to speak. All that came out of his mouth was a croak like that of a frog. Hands helped him sit up. A cup was placed in his hands.

"Toast water," a gravelly voice said from behind him. "Slow now."

Louis sipped until his thirst was gone and the cup half empty.

"Hungry?" a softer voice asked.

He nodded. The cup was replaced with a bowl of porridge. He lifted the warm gruel to his mouth, one slow spoonful at a time. He'd never felt so hungry before. He looked back to see who had been helping him. Two nurses stood there. One was a bald-headed gray-beard who looked to be in his sixties and the other a big raw-boned woman with a hooked nose.

"Thank you," he croaked. Suddenly his stomach cramped as if it were caught in a vise. "Have to . . ." he said, grabbing his belly.

The two understood. They helped him from his smelly cot. His nose was working again. It was hard to endure his own stench. The cot was badly soiled. He hoped it would get cleaned while he was out of it.

The old male nurse was half the size of the hook-nosed woman, but he was the one who helped Louis limp out of the tent. Louis was glad of that. Despite all the awful things they must see every day, they were trying to help him keep a little dignity.

Had he been on his own and whole, not stumbling and almost falling with each step, it would have been easy enough to find the latrine pit by himself. The stench that rose from the sink was complemented by swarms of flies that circled him like a cloud. He crouched over the pole, the man holding him under both arms.

"Appears you ain't got the trots," the gray-bearded nurse said, nodding in approval. "Thank God for that, son. Once you get the dysentery, there's only two ways to go. One is that they start giving you laudanum. Though it stems the flow, you end up wanting more and more of that opium till it's all you live for. The other is that it just empties your whole insides out till there's nothing left. For every man jack dies of wounds, two more that perishes from the Virginia quick-step. Now let's get you back in. You need any help, jes' call fer Jake."

Another day passed before the doctor came back again to probe at Louis's wounds with that dirty finger.

That bothered Louis. Not just the pain of it. His mother had told him that dirt must always be kept out of even the smallest cuts. Louis remembered the times his mother had taken him with her to carry her bag and sit outside the door. She always washed her hands clean with water and herbs before binding someone's wounds or going in to a woman at her birthing time.

The doctor shook his head. "No pus. Bad sign." He cleared his throat and spat on the ground. Then he was gone again.

I should have asked him about my company. I should have asked someone.

Jake was back that afternoon.

"I need to ask you something," Louis said. "I was at Reams Station, Company E of the Sixty-ninth."

"Oh my," Jake said. "I heered about that. You wants to know of your buddies, don't you?"

Louis nodded.

"Well, you boys took an awful mauling there. Gimme their names. I'll jes' ask and see if any you might know is hereabouts."

Yet another day. No word of his friends, but his strength returning.

Merci, Bon Dieu. I get to the latrine on my own now.

Jake was pleased at that.

"You don't go regular," Jake said, "our doctors'll start you on the calomel. That's their favorite dose here. But you don't want that, boy." His voice lowered to a whisper. "I'm no doctor—haven't kilt enough men to be one—but I've seen enough to know that jes' as sure as the day is long you do not want the calomel. It's made of mercury and sugar of lead. Your teeth start coming out after a week and your jawbone falls in on itself. Bad medicine, that."

CHAPTER THIRTY-FOUR
THE ANGEL

I should be getting well faster.

That thought ate at him like a worm in an apple.

How long has it been?

Hard to keep track of the passage of time. The first part of his stay had been a fog. Though he was eating solid food now, most days all he could do was lie on his cot with his eyes closed, his hand to his forehead. Had a week passed?

He'd had special visitors twice. The first was a new lieutenant of the 69th. No one he'd ever met before and he forgot the name. The officer had complimented him on his bravery. He was getting some sort of medal for bravery. Maybe two medals. He didn't much care about that. All he cared about was how the others made out.

The answer had given him some satisfaction.

"Let me check," the new lieutenant replied, looking through the papers he carried, running a finger down a column. "Appears you and a Private Belaney—poor lad lost a leg—are the only two who stayed at Depot Hospital for any time."

"Sergeant Flynn?" Louis asked.

The lieutenant smiled. "Ah. I've made his acquaintance. He's the one put you in for the ribbons. Sends his greetings. Minor flesh wound. Bullet grazed his head. He's been given a three-week leave to convalesce at home."

"Cook? Devlin? Kirk?"

"Not in my list of casualties."

"Corporal Hayes?"

The new lieutenant's face darkened. "Missing, I'm afraid. Assumed dead or captured. Sorry about that."

The second visit, a day or so later, had been from The Angel.

That was what they called her—not just the sick and wounded, but the nurses as well. A ripple of excited voices marked her approach.

"The Angel's here!"

"She's come down to visit!"

It was one of his bad days. He didn't sit up or open his eyes, just kept pressing his hand to his forehead to try and make the aching stop. Then he felt a warm presence. Someone was kneeling by his cot. A smell as sweet as spring flowers was replacing the awful odors of illness and death that were never gone, even from an open-air tent.

"Young soldier," a strong, clear voice spoke.

A small, firm hand slid in to replace Louis's own on his forehead. He opened his eyes to look up into the round, handsome face of a small woman. Her expression was as caring as a mother looking at her own sick child. She had a bottle in her other hand and was sprinkling it around her and his cot.

"Lavender water," the woman explained. "My name is Clara Barton."

Clara Barton.

Louis knew her name. So did everyone in the army.

The Angel of the Battlefield herself.

Louis had read about her. She'd left a good job in the U.S. Patent Office to tend the wounded at Second Bull Run. So few doctors and so little planning for casualties in those early days of the war that Clara with her wagonload of food and her own medical supplies had been the first to arrive. Cooking, comforting the injured, caring for their wounds herself, that was what Clara Barton did then and was still doing.

"What is your name, young man?"

"Louis."

"Louis," Clara Barton repeated. "A fine name for a brave young soldier." Her hand was still on his forehead. For the first time in days Louis felt his headache diminishing. He started to smile—his lips trembling as he did so. It was the first time he'd really smiled since the battle at the railroad.

"Where were you wounded?"

Louis wondered for a moment why she couldn't see the

bandages on his legs and arms, then realized she was asking about the place.

"Reams Station," he said.

Clara Barton nodded. "A very bad one. But you came through."

She moved her hand across his forehead and as she did so Louis saw a hole in the long sleeve of her black dress.

"Ah," she said, noticing where his gaze had strayed. She put down her bottle of lavender water to touch the hole in her garment with her other hand. "I have never mended this and I never shall. A bullet passed through there, killing the man I was tending."

She smiled, but it didn't go beyond her lips.

Mon Dieu, she is sad.

Clara Barton shook her sleeve back down. "Of course, I do not need it as a reminder of what war is about. I have seen too often that it is not conquering armies, but boys like yourself toiling in the rain and darkness with no thought of pride or glory or reward, their faces bathed in tears and their hands in blood." Clara Barton sighed. "There is no need for me to make a speech to you. I only pray that you shall grow well and strong again."

She pressed his forehead again with her hand, rose, and was gone.

But I haven't grown well and strong again.

Louis shook his head in near despair. He'd been getting

weaker every day since The Angel's visit. He slid his hand, which was too heavy to lift, down toward his leg.

No doubt about it. Hot to the touch.

Plus his nose had begun picking up a smell from his wound.

The doctor looked graver than usual as he did his customary painful poking and prodding.

Louis heard the words he spoke to one of the nurses as he walked away.

"I haven't the time now to do it, but that leg will have to come off this afternoon. It won't take long. Fifteen minutes at the most."

I'd rather die.

A wry smile twisted his face.

With this doctor's care I probably will.

He began to think about his death.

What will it be like? Will I walk the road of stars that leads up into the skyland? Will I see my father again? Will one of those angels that Father Andre spoke to me about come down and open its great white wings to embrace me? I wish . . .

But Louis never finished that thought. The sound of a commotion reached his ears.

"You cannot . . ."

"You're not allowed . . ."

"Madame!"

"*Nda! Allez!* You will not stop me."

"Hands off the lady," a second voice said.

Louis knew that second voice. It was Artis. It made his heart

273

leap, but what filled him with even more joy was that he had also recognized the woman's voice he heard first.

Only one person in the world could sound as fierce and loving as that or speak such a mix of Indian and French and English. Another sort of angel had just arrived for him.

"M'mere," Louis sobbed as Artis helped him to sit up. Then he was in Marie Nolette's strong arms.

CHAPTER THIRTY-FIVE
HEALING

*T*here was no logical way—as far as white man's logic went—for his mother to have known he needed her. No one had written her a letter about his injuries. No one sent a telegram to the Indian mother of one insignificant private.

Yet her long journey south began on the day Louis fell at Reams Station.

When I called for her to come and help me.

"The trees," M'mere said. "They tell me you need me. So I come."

Things have to be done according to the rules in the army. Regulations have to be followed. Louis had learned that in the months he'd been a soldier. But even the army found it hard to resist Marie Nolette. After marching across four states carrying a bag nearly as big as herself on her back, she was not about to be deterred by rules, regulations, or those who thought they could enforce them when faced by one small French Canadian Indian mother.

The first one she confounded was the doctor. As M'mere held Louis, he returned with his saw and two attendants to carry Louis to the operating table.

M'mere snatched the saw from him and threw it on the ground!

"You man with dirty hands! *Nda!* You will take my head before you touch his leg."

As the doctor and his two helpers backed off from his mother, who looked more like a female wolverine than a human, Louis caught a glimpse of Jake, the male nurse. Jake grinned like a jack-o'-lantern and held up both thumbs.

The next was a corporal who tried to explain that there was no way a mother could just sweep in and take her son with her. Although a patient, Private Nolette was still a soldier.

"And you have used him up," Marie said. "Now you go to cut off his leg. So what use will he be as a soldier? Him you do not need. You give him back to me."

Louis watched openmouthed. He hadn't realized how well his mother could speak the English language that she always said stuck in her throat like a fish bone.

The cowed corporal was replaced by a sergeant who ended up shaking his head and going for a lieutenant. By now a crowd of soldiers on crutches, nurses, and orderlies had formed around the tent.

"I will stay here to fight for my son if it take me all summer!" Marie Nolette said, standing beside his cot and crossing her arms on her chest. She turned to wink at Louis to let him know her choice of words had been no accident.

"You tell him, ma'am!" a soldier leaning on two canes shouted out from the bandages that covered most of his face.

"They ain't gonna back her down!" a one-armed private chipped in, pumping his remaining fist in the air.

A loud *Hurrah!* went up from the crowd as the befuddled lieutenant retired from the field of battle. This was the best entertainment that had ever come to Depot Hospital.

My mother!

There was so much hope and pride in his heart now that Louis thought it might burst. He was grinning as widely as all the others who'd gathered to take his mother's side.

The captain, who was the last to arrive, came with a handful of papers.

Louis's mother took half a step forward, her chin up, her index finger raised. Before she could speak, the officer raised his hand in a conciliatory manner.

"Mrs. Nolette," the captain said, in an extremely polite voice, "we've looked into your son's records. He's due to be honored with several commendations, it seems. Wouldn't you like to see him stay here to get his medals?"

"You want him to have medals, you send them to him, eh?" Marie Nolette pressed her lips together and nodded.

The captain nodded back to her.

The man is trying not to laugh. He's smart enough to be as amused by this as everyone else—except that sawbones.

Louis could see the doctor out of the corner of his eye. Clearly displeased, he'd been pushed to the back of the crowd—hopefully holding the dirty saw he'd retrieved from the muddy tent floor.

"In that case," the captain said, handing the papers to Louis's mother, "if you accept the consequences of removing him from professional hands, we're placing your son in your care."

The captain produced a pen. "Just make your mark here, ma'am."

Artis helped him to his feet, wrapping a blanket around his shoulders. Louis's head was spinning even more than it had been from his fever. People were cheering, patting him on the back, grasping his hands.

"Good luck to you, laddie."

"'Bout time somebody on our side had a victory."

"Your ma'd make a better general than the sorry lot we been saddled with!"

Then they were in the sunshine outside the tent, Artis supporting him with an arm around his shoulders on one side, M'mere under Louis's arm to his left.

"*Nigawes,* my mother, I have no clothes for traveling."

"In my bag," Marie Nolette replied.

A cheer went up from somewhere behind the tent they'd just left.

Louis turned to look. Near the back of the crowd Jake cupped his hands to shout to Louis.

"Had a little ac-cy-dent back here. Doc fell into the sinkhole!"

The elation that gave him strength began to fade as they moved away from Depot Hospital. They were on one of the roads now that led up from the river.

Don't know if I can take another step.

A wagon pulled up next to them.

"Sorry I'm late, ma'am," a bearded wagoneer said to Louis's mother.

Artis slipped his arm from around Louis's shoulders. "Grab hold."

Louis grasped the side of the wagon to steady himself.

His mother wrapped her arms around Artis. Louis could see from the surprised look on his Mohawk friend's face how much strength Marie Nolette was putting into that hug.

Bet she cracked at least two of his ribs, Louis thought as his mother let loose and Artis took a deep breath.

His mother whispered a few words and then put something in Artis's hand. He nodded and slipped the medicine she'd given him for protection into his pocket.

The tall Mohawk boy turned back to Louis.

"Far as I go, brother," Artis said. He squeezed Louis's shoulder and stepped back. "You travel well. Your ma will take care of you. From what I have seen of her, she can cure everything except that bad case of the Abenaki uglies you got."

Artis looked up for a minute, took a deep breath, then reached down to his belt. He untied the bag of marbles and placed them in Louis's hand. "I'll win these back from you after the war."

Then Artis walked away without looking back.

Should of told him that no Abenaki ever beat a Mohawk in an ugly contest.

But the moment had passed. Artis had taken his leave in true Indian fashion.

We don't have words for good-bye.

"Climb on," the yellow-bearded driver said.

As soon as they were settled in, his mother cut off the moist dressings.

"Wet bandages! Fools! Do they not know you must keep a wound dry."

She reached into her bag and brought out a flask filled with brown liquid.

"Drink," she said.

Louis drank, warmth spreading from his throat through his chest. He breathed in and out, each breath bringing him a little more strength.

His mother held out a pair of moccasins. She helped him pull off his boots, threw them into the back of the wagon as he put the soft moose skin slippers on his feet. He lay back and his mother wrapped the blanket around him.

It was dark when the wagoneer dropped them off in the countryside.

Where are we? These woods look as thick as it was in the Wilderness.

His mother helped him down. Easier to walk with moccasins on his feet, though his leg ached some. She led him along a barely visible trail through the brush. It came out in a large clearing. Canvas-covered huts made of brush and bent saplings were mixed in with small log cabins in a circle around a central fire.

"*Nidobak,*" his mother said. "Friends."

People with brown faces came up to them. Some wore clothing made of skin. Others were dressed like Southern farmers.

Indians, Louis thought.

Their words sounded like Abenaki, but the accent was strange. He was led into a cabin, placed on a bed.

An old man, his face as lined as a map, looked at the open wound in his leg, the one that smelled of gangrene. He and M'mere nodded heads in agreement.

The old man went outside. When he returned it was with a bark cup that he handed to M'mere. She carefully reached in, began to place the contents of the cup along the edges of the wound in his thigh where flesh had begun to rot. Small things the size of white beans. They squirmed as she held them. Maggots.

The old man patted Louis's shoulder, said something in Indian. Because of the accent, it took Louis a minute to understand.

Clean good. Eat sickness away.

He nodded and closed his eyes.

A deep, loud sound woke him.

Cannons!

He sat up from his blankets, heart pounding, reaching for the rifle that should have been by his side. But his Springfield wasn't there.

Where?

His mother's hands grasped his shoulders, gently pushing him back down.

"The fever, she is gone," M'mere whispered. "*Oligawi.* Sleep good."

Louis relaxed. He remembered where he was.

Not guns. The rumble of thunder.

A smile came to his lips. Things on this earth were continuing as the great good spirit Ktsi Nwaskw meant them to continue. Despite wars and all the foolishness of men, the Thunder Being, who cleansed the earth from evil, was walking again across the sky.

CHAPTER THIRTY-SIX

ABOVE THE TOWN

$\mathscr{A}$s Louis sat in the bent wood chair he'd finished making that morning, he looked out over the land. Fields and woods and in the distance the blue haze of the Green Mountains of Vermont. What M'mere had said in her letters had turned out to be true. Fishing was good in the pond. Pickerel, perch, bullhead. The farm had fine fertile ground for growing corn and beans and potatoes. Plenty of good trees. And this view...

You surely can see a wide swath of God's Creation from the top of Cole Hill.

It was especially beautiful today, now that the first frost had touched the sugar maples. The land was a patchwork of gold and scarlet sewn in among the green of pine and spruce and cedar and hemlock. He looked at the crutches leaning against the wall of their small cabin. A spider had set up shop between them. The harvest of dried fly carcasses at the bottom edge of the web showed that it had been doing good business at its prime location for some time now.

Louis stretched out his leg. The scar pulled a little, but his limb was as strong as it had been before.

Fit to chase down a deer by the moon when the leaves fall.

As he thought that, a feeling of guilt swept over him.

He walked to the southeast corner of the porch. At night the valley below was dark save for a few scattered lights from farmsteads. Louis thought back on those nights when he'd looked from high places to see the glow of countless thousands of army campfires, the lights of the Rebels' camp across the line like a reflection.

I pray to God I never see such a sight from this hill.

He touched the hip pocket where he'd put the letter. It arrived for him at the post office in the Greenfield General Store a week ago, but he'd just picked it up yesterday.

M'mere must have told him where he could reach us.

Louis pulled it out, unfolded it, and read it for the tenth time.

> Deer Louis,
> Things iz quiet here. Rebs iz wore out, it semz. Nothin to do in camp but ete, play cardz and get fat. So I take pencil in

hand and rite you these words. The boys
all say hello to you. Joker wants to know
if you are still az ugly as you was and
I tole him that since you are back home
and likely eatin much bark you are probly
uglier even. Ho ho. Songbird haz got his
voice back, which iz good since I em tired
of herin some of the new boys in our compny
try to sing. The sergent sens hiz best
regards. Sad news iz that there iz no
sure news bout Hayes, though the sergent
thinks he may be at Andersonvil. I hope
not. You stil got my marbls?

Faithfully yerz,
Mr. Artis Leander Cook

Louis walked back to the chair and sat again. It was time
he had some employment, now that he was all healed up.
It wasn't right that M'mere should be the only one earning
money—though he was still drawing his pay and could apply
for a pension as a disabled soldier.

Except I'm not. I'm fit as a fiddle.

He thought about what it would be like that night. His

birthday supper. He'd finally turned sixteen. Only sixteen. After all he'd seen, he felt like it ought to be sixty. He was a long way from the killing fields of Virginia, but even further away from the boy he'd been. He woke up every night missing the feel of his Springfield next to him. Despite his mother's remedies, he still had bad dreams.

Azonis and her parents and her brothers would be at dinner that night. She was no longer a little girl for sure. He saw the two of them marrying and settling down. He smiled at the thought of the way Azonis looked at him. As if he was some sort of hero.

Not a man who'd deserted his friends.

Louis sighed. He knew how they'd react when he told them tonight.

No.

You already done your duty.

Strong as she was, his mother would cry. But she'd realize that her son, who was just as stubborn as his father, had made up his mind.

Are you certain sure?

Louis raised his eyes beyond the hills. He saw in his mind those Virginia mountains, those tidal rivers, that terrible beautiful landscape he realized he couldn't leave behind just yet.

He held up Artis's letter.

"Be seeing you boys soon," he whispered to the wind.

*Louis's journey
through the battles of the
Irish Brigade's Virginia Campaign
in the summer of 1864*

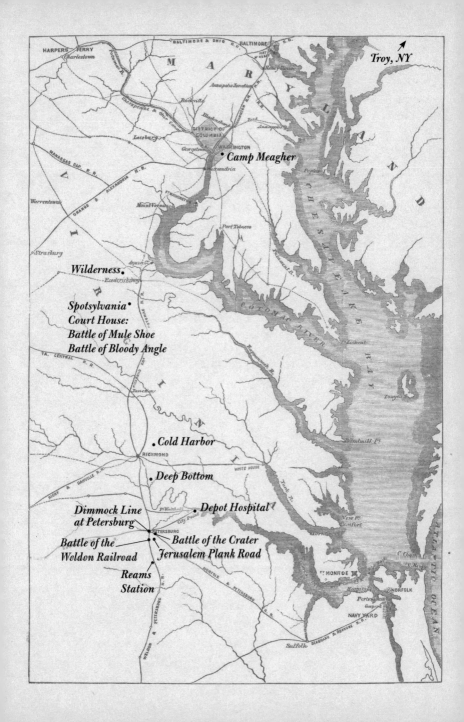

Troy, NY

Camp Meagher

Wilderness

Spotsylvania
Court House:
Battle of Mule Shoe
Battle of Bloody Angle

Cold Harbor

Deep Bottom

Depot Hospital

Dimmock Line
at Petersburg

Battle of the Crater

Battle of the
Weldon Railroad

Jerusalem Plank Road

Reams
Station

AUTHOR'S NOTE

$\mathscr{T}$his novel is deeply rooted in fact. The events it describes in the Civil War, the weaponry, the military terms, the language used by the characters, the food they eat, even the songs they sing, are all real and the result of many years of research on my part.

Although the protagonist and his closest companions are fictional, all of the other characters and events are from the historical record. Plus, though I chose to call my main character by a different name, Louis Nolette is based on my own great-grandfather, an Abenaki Indian from Canada who did serve in the Irish Brigade in 1864.

Like many Americans, I've always felt a close connection to this war. When I was a child, my family drove south each summer to spend time with my great-uncle—my grandmother's brother Orvis Dunham. A Northerner, he had chosen to live in Virginia, where he managed the Warm Springs Hotel. Our stops along the way always included Gettysburg, Pennsylvania, where we would tour the battlefield, and Washington, D.C., where we visited museums and historical sites. We always knew when we crossed the Mason-Dixon Line, for it was a segregated South that we entered back then. The gas stations had separate drinking fountains for White and Colored. My grandfather Jesse Bowman, whose own Indian skin was the darkest in our family, only made that trip with us once after being told by a gas station attendant that he could not use the restroom with the sign WHITES ONLY on its door.

In Virginia, Great-Uncle Orvis took us on more battlefield tours, reliving stories he'd learned from men who'd survived those grim struggles. He also took us to visit African American friends who'd been his employees at the big hotel, bringing them food or presents for their children. Their shacks were a sad contrast to the homes of white Virginians. If the war had really been fought to free the slaves, I remember thinking back then, then why were things still this way in Virginia? Although it all happened long before I was born, the American Civil War was never just a distant memory to me.

My grandfather Jesse Bowman's own father, Louis Bowman, was a Civil War veteran. But I knew little about it. Grampa Jesse told me that his father would never say anything about his experience in the war. It was better not told. But the memories of it were always with him, for he'd been gravely wounded and left for dead on the battlefield. "When I told him I'd enlisted for World War I," my grandfather told me, "my father broke down and cried."

I knew that my great-grandfather had served in a New York regiment, but I didn't know that much about the details of his service until my sister Margaret, our family's best historian and most dogged researcher, came to my aid as she always does. (You'll find Marge credited in the author's notes of many of my historical novels.) Among other things, she managed to get the pension records from the National Archives of our great-grandfather, listed not as Louis, but "Lewis" Bowman. Despite the discrepancy in the first name, there was no doubt from the details that it was he.

Soldier's certificate # 208738

Lewis Bowman

5' 8¹/₂", dark complexion, dark hair, black eyes

born in Canada

farmer and laborer

resident of Porter's Corners

Town of Greenfield, Saratoga

recruited by Captain Forsythe at East Troy, New York

Private, Company E, 69th New York Infantry

Commander Peter W. Sweeney

Medical discharge August 14, 1865 at Stanton General Hospital, Washington, DC

My great-grandfather was Canadian, but a Canadian of Native descent whose ancestral roots were in what became the United States. Records list his birth place as St. Francis, the name then used for the Abenaki Indian reserve of Odanak, a mission village made up largely of refugee Indians from New England who fled north to escape the English during the eighteenth century. (I've written about the eighteenth-century experiences of Odanak Abenakis in two of my earlier novels, *The Arrow Over the Door* and *The Winter People*.) Like numerous other young Canadian Indian men, my great-grandfather came south to find work because little was available around the reserve.

And, in 1864, it was in the United States that a recruiter for the Irish Brigade found him.

THE IRISH BRIGADE

*D*uring the Civil War, it is estimated that more than 150,000 Irishmen fought for the Union. There was also an entire Southern brigade of Irishmen that fought on the side of the Confederacy. Why was this so? The answers can be found in recent Irish history.

Despite centuries of struggle against British rule, throughout the nineteenth century Ireland was still a colonial possession of England. Although Irish men and women had already been coming to the United States for many years in large numbers, the greatest influx of Irish immigrants occurred in 1846, as a result of a blight that destroyed the Irish potato crop in 1845. In one of the greatest disasters in history, the population of Ireland dropped from about 8.5 million to 6.5 million. Many starved, but an estimated 1,600,000 Irish men and women came to the United States.

These new immigrants were generally not welcomed. They were Catholic in what was then a largely Protestant nation. They were competing for scarce jobs in a struggling economy. Many refused to hire anyone with an Irish name. Signs reading NO IRISH NEED APPLY began to appear in American cities.

In 1851, well before the Civil War, the Irish citizens of New York City formed a volunteer militia that was accepted as part of the New York State Militia as the 69th Regiment. After the attack on Fort Sumter, the 69th, led by Colonel Michael Corcoran, fought at the first battle of Bull Run, serving as the rear guard during the Union retreat. Two more New York regiments that were mostly Irish, the 63rd New York and the 88th New York, and two other regiments, the 28th Massachusetts and the 116th Pennsylvania, were added to the 69th to form the Irish Brigade.

With a lack of opportunity for other jobs, the example of prominent Irish Americans, the generous cash bonuses being offered to recruits . . . it's not surprising that many Irish jumped at the chance to enlist. Moreover, by the mid-nineteenth century the Irish already had a long and honorable history of military service, having signed on as mercenary soldiers in wars all over the European continent. Becoming a soldier was a familiar path for a young Irishman with no other road to take. Although the cash bonuses offered for volunteering were attractive, their motives were not just monetary. Some saw it as a way to gain military experience that they might use when the American Civil War was won, in a later battle to free their own homeland from British rule.

There is no doubt too that after years of struggle against "English despotism" that made the proud Irish people feel like slaves, many identified with the Union cause. A recruiting advertisement that appeared in the *Boston Herald* on July 30, 1862, begins with these words, which appeal to that Irish pride and patriotism:

> *"Shall villains drag our starry flag*
> *By the blood of warriors consecrated*
> *And raise instead the viper's head*
> *O'er Northern freemen subjugated?*
> *No, no, the boasts of Southern hosts*
> *By heaven right soon we'll make them swallow,*
> *They'll shortly feel our Yankee steel*
> *Backed by an Irish Faugh au Ballaghs."*

Faugh au Ballaghs is a Gaelic phrase that means "Clear the way." It became the battle cry of the largely Irish regiments that became known as the Irish Brigade, men who combined the pride of being Irish with their desire to fight for freedom. In large part, the men of the Irish Brigade lived up to that motto. They were usually the first into battle where the fighting was the worst. By the end of the war, no other Brigade had been more praised for gallantry, dash, and discipline. They also suffered the third-highest casualty rate in the Union army. Of the 7,715 men who served in its ranks, over 4,000 were killed or mortally wounded.

Riamh Nar Dhruid O Saprin lann. Those words, also in Gaelic, mean "Who never retreated from the clash of spears." They were emblazoned on a field of green, under a sunburst and an Irish harp, on the regimental colors of the 69th New York, that first and most famous of the five regiments that made up the Irish Brigade. Their nickname, the "Fighting 69th," was given them by none other than Confederate General Robert E. Lee, who was less than pleased whenever he saw their green flag facing his lines.

Because their losses were always so great, the Irish Brigade went through several periods of major recruitment. One of them was in the early part of 1864. And although the Brigade was still mostly Irish, other men who had been common laborers, men from communities with an equal lack of opportunity, joined up. Some were American Indians, some were Canadians, and some, like my own great-grandfather, were both.

Selected Bibliography

I read hundreds of volumes in researching this novel. Here are a few I found especially useful and interesting, books that should also be helpful for any reader wishing to know more about the history behind my story.

Between Two Fires: American Indians in the Civil War by Laurence M. Hauptman. New York: The Free Press, 1995.

The Civil War Day by Day: An Almanac 1861–1865 by E. B. Long with Barbara Long. New York: Da Capo Press, 1971.

Civil War Weapons and Equipment by Russ A. Pritchard Jr. Guilford, CT: The Lyons Press, 2003.

The Complete Idiot's Guide to the Civil War by Alan Axelrod. New York: Alpha Books, 2003.

The Everything Civil War Book by Donald Vaughn. Holbrook, MA: Adams Media, 2000.

The Irish Brigade and Its Campaigns by David Power Conyngham, edited by Lawrence Frederick Kohl. New York: Fordham University Press, 1994.

The Life of Billy Yank: the Common Soldier of the Union by Bell Irvin Wiley. Baton Rouge: Louisiana State University Press, 1978.

The Life of Johnny Reb: the Common Soldier of the Confederacy by Bell Irvin Wiley. Baton Rouge: Louisiana State University Press, 1978.

The Negro's Civil War by James M. McPherson. New York: Vintage Books Civil War Library, 2003.

They Fought Like Demons: Women Soldiers in the Civil War by DeAnne Blanton and Lauren M. Cook. New York: Vintage Books, 2002.

Warrior in Two Camps: Ely S. Parker, Union General and Seneca Chief by William H. Armstrong. Syracuse, NY: Syracuse University Press, 1978.

What They Didn't Teach You About the Civil War by Mike Wright. New York: Ballantine Books, 1996.